Don't Bang the Barista!

Leigh Matthews

To Carly and Maya, and beleaguered baristas
everywhere.

CHAPTER ONE

I smiled, admiring the heart shape formed in foam atop my latte. Looking up, I tried to catch the eye of the woman who had, a minute earlier, scooched my coffee across the counter but the lovely barista had already moved on and was smiling solicitously at the enplaided early-twenty-something next in line. I suppressed a sad exhalation, wedged my water bottle under my arm, picked up the saucer, and stepped gingerly back to the table where Cass was waiting. Her withering look was in full bloom.

"Give it up already," Cass said.

"What?"

"You know. Don't pretend like your face isn't as red as your high-tops right now. She's not interested in you. She's just doing her job."

"But look at her, Cass. Look! At! Her!" I sighed audibly this time and sipped at my drink, trying not to disturb the foam heart and going cross-eyed as I checked its integrity with each motion of my lips.

"Kate, honey, you know the first rule of coffee-shop dating..."

The two of us uttered the same sentence, me in a begrudging murmur, Cass laughingly.

"Don't Bang the Barista."

I put down my cup and picked up the legwarmer I was halfway through knitting for Em, focusing on reacquiring the stitches that had slipped off the needle in my bag. I started to knit a row, silent for a moment. Then, closing my eyes tight, I dropped the knitting next to my drink. After a couple of seconds of shutting out the world, I looked up at my friend.

"It's alright for you though," I said, "you're fine just ripping through every queer in town. I want to find someone to adopt fucking rescue pigs with. That's a pretty unique proposition. It's not just a case of 'are they fuckable' and do they own enough Amber Dawn books to spark a brief conversation pre-shag."

Cass laughed. "That's both the most and the least British thing I've heard today."

I gave her the stiff-upper-lip-stare.

"Look," Cass said, "you're just trying too hard, and expecting too much too soon. No one is going to match all of your criteria so just find someone to have fun with and stop being so serious."

"You really do not understand me at all, do you? Why are we friends again?" I smiled lopsidedly.

"Because I let you beat me at Scrabble and you charm me with your excited commentary on acquiring vegan roving and a spinning wheel." Cass pushed her tortoiseshell-framed glasses back up her nose and drank the last of her Americano. "I have to get to class. We're discussing conspicuous othering in 20th Century American literature. Fuck me."

"Can I come?"

"Nope. You have work to do. I know you do, so stop sitting there with a sour face. And no more

2

mooning over Hanna." Cass stood up and started for the door.

"Wait! You know her name?!" My so-called friend looked over her shoulder and winked, then headed outside to retrieve her bike.

Great, I thought, Cass has probably already slept with the barista and is only just now telling me. Is there anyone in this city who has not dated or slept with someone I know? Not that having slept with a friend or acquaintance automatically rules people out, of course. Maybe. Or does it? If they've been rejected by a friend then why would I want to date them seriously? I felt the seemingly inevitable brain spiral coming on, playing out the same tired logic that had been filling my head for months now. I tried to skip to the end; the part where I eventually realised that, yada yada yada, everyone's needs are different and what works in a relationship for one person doesn't necessarily work for everyone else. It doesn't help to know that though. Not when I'm looking at Hanna and thinking about how much better in bed I bet Cass is and how even if I got to that point with her she'd be comparing me to Cass and come away disappointed. Was it time for a beer yet? It was only 10.30. Today was not starting out well.

I opened up my laptop and tapped in the password, thinking once again about how I should really change it to something less embarrassing in case anyone ever needed to know it. It's been the same for two years, just as my banking passwords are the same, and my PINs. I never change. Maybe this year, this month, hell, even today should be different? What would happen if I just changed everything? If I just started behaving like Cass instead of myself, would I be happier or just more chafed and always out of laundry money? I stood up and walked back to the counter, my gaze firmly fixed on Hanna. She turned and smiled, raising her eyebrows a little in question.

"Er, could I... ah. Would you... happen to have a pen I could borrow? Mine just ran out of ink and I'm, well, I'm supposed to be making notes on a thing and, um." I am not Cass. I am not suave. I am a damp, distressed, dolt.

Hanna handed me a pen, biting her lip in amusement and turning back to the stack of coffee bean bags she had been checking off on an invoice. She hadn't said a word. She hadn't needed to.

CHAPTER TWO

I sat down on a bench at the top of China Creek Park and wondered if I had time to go and snuggle puppies at the nearby SPCA before Em arrived. Probably not. Instead, I watched the crows head back to Burnaby for the night, momentarily darkening the sky. The man on the next bench over was playing a saxophone, casting music down into the belly of the park where a bunch of elementary school kids were kicking around a football, all youthful spunk and high-vis vests. One of the kids was pretty good, Cruyff turns and all. I bet all the other kids hated him. Maybe he was bad at math or something though. Just to even things out.

God. I need a girlfriend. I had become so bitter and full of resentment. How did that happen? When did everyone else get so fucking happy and my life turned to shit? I was enjoying this brief moment of despair, set to the soulful sax, when Em plopped down on the bench next to me.

"'Sup? You look like you're about to go all *Carrie* on those kids down there. Is the music stirring up some deep-seated childhood memories? Did your mom force you to practice the saxophone until your fingers bled when all you wanted to do was play soccer?"

In this moment I decided that not only did I need a girlfriend, I also needed better friends. There was only so much banter a girl could take. Why did no one see my existential crisis for what it really was? I turned to Em, forgetting to even say hi.

"Am I a joke to all of you?"

Em looked at me, stunned, then smiled, scrunched up her eyes and asked, "Kaaaate... what's going on?"

I swallowed down the bile that had forced its way up my gullet, sliding around on the back of my tongue. Gritting my teeth, I flashed a brief and unconvincing smile at my oldest friend, at least my oldest friend in this country. I opened my mouth to speak and just couldn't think of any words that worked any more. There was just sadness. Too much fucking sadness.

Em took my hand. The pattern on her gloves began to waver as my eyes filled with tears that wouldn't fall. Not yet. She murmured, "Oh, sweetie." Then the tears fell and the words fell too.

"What am I doing wrong, Em? Everything is just collapsing around me and I can't stop it and no one good is going to be drawn to that. I've created this gravity, this fucking vortex of doom that is sucking more bad shit in and anyone with any sense is just going to stay the fuck away from me."

Em stroked my hand and put her other arm around my shoulder. "All you need is a..."

Nice cup of tea?

A good fuck?

A sense of reason?

"... A bit of time. You've had a tough year and you're being too hard on yourself. You're awesome and this is just a wobble and it'll all be fine. Just give yourself

6

some..." Please Em, please don't say it... "Some critical space." Fuck.

I had known Em since 2010, after meeting her at a vegan potluck thing organised by a, now disbanded, Meetup group. We had both ended up lurking in a corner in the kitchen, wondering if it was appropriate to reveal the sparkling wine we had each brought in case of mimosa potential. Of course, we only realised this later because we were both so paralysed by impropriety that we ended up drinking the wine at our respective homes in a fit of self-loathing later in the day. I didn't even have juice with mine. Em was no doubt more organised.

Over the past three years her life had changed quite a bit. Graduating from the MA that she had been working on for four years and finally joining the workforce and realising how little she missed going to class and reading papers and analysing shit. She hadn't even gone into social justice work as she'd planned. Instead, she'd ended up at a PR company writing witty little slogans for products she despised but found captivatingly awful in some cheery way. I figured she was due a crash soon and would rediscover those political roots and that longing for action but maybe she deserved to just pay off some of that debt first with an easy paycheck.

Em had also found love; a guy a little older than her, which had surprised a lot of her queer friends but not me because I hadn't known her with anyone else and they seemed to just fit perfectly, hosting their clever little dinner parties with real wine glasses, not just Mason jars. They were talking about getting a dog and I wondered if that was code for turning their spare room into a nursery in a year or so. One nugget of knowledge gleaned from many an hour in the dog park: You can pretty much guess the age of the Labrador or Golden Retriever by how old the child is running alongside. A two year old toddler, huh? I bet you that dog is three, and a bit disgruntled.

Where was I? Critical space. Oh Em.

Space wasn't the problem. I was.

If only I could figure out how to get space from myself.

"You know, I tried to ask out the barista from Our Town and I ended up asking her for a pen."

"What?"

"Nothing. Let's go and get a beer at Barney's before we head over for the show." I wiped at my eyes with the sleeve of my coat and checked my phone. No messages. I wondered if Cass would be at the Biltmore tonight. I had a feeling she'd probably know a couple of the bands playing and would make her way over. Em hadn't met Cass yet and seemed to think that I'd fallen for her a bit. Cass is super cute and smart and funny but, having seen her tripping out on acid in the morning sunshine in the dog park, any romantic shine was gone. She is cute though. Damn.

CHAPTER THREE

The line-up outside the Biltmore was almost to the Kingsway corner when Em and I arrived. I left Em at the back of the queue and I walked down to see if there was anyone I knew. There's a certain awkwardness to walking the line, trying not to peer too hard into faces covered by hats and scarves.

I was listening for laughs and screeches, looking for fancy socks and a cluster of tiny lesbians although I figured they'd have told me if they were going to be at the gig tonight, probably. I got to the front and saw Cass sharing a spliff with the security guy, his broken Italian English making her look at him sideways. I knew that look. She did it when she didn't get my accent and I had to paraphrase quickly to keep the conversational flow. It had become a well-practised habit, deliberately choosing words that sounded right to the Canadian ear and avoiding those that marked me out as foreign.

I had never enjoyed loud spaces, being unable to pick out voices. Now, though, I really disliked them as I could tell that half of what I said was misheard or not heard at all. It's funny how people think foreign accents are sexy. Yeah, it's totally sexy not to have any clue what someone is saying to you. At least tonight's gig was a little more low-key; four solo performers followed by a more rousing band of folk musicians.

I didn't know anyone who was playing, but Em had wanted to come because she'd been working so much recently that she'd gotten into a routine of going home and collapsing into the couch every night. She'd said that she and Steve had reached that point where they were worried about being stuck in a rut, not realising that, to me, a well-worn groove sounded pretty nice right about now. "We need to spend time apart, remembering things that interest us, aside from each other!" Em had said.

I was happy to play the single stooge as I'd missed her in recent months, never able to bring the desired dinner date to make up the numbers and always feeling like I was ripe for being set up at every party. Em had lost a few friends when she and Steve got together - a strange form of heterophobia, it seemed. She was rarely invited to burlesque or queer dance parties or even knit-ins any more, not through conspicuous avoidance, just out of an odd anxiety over making Steve feel awkward and unwanted. Yes, the irony was awful. I also wondered at how much many of my friends were desirous of a queer-only space and whether having such a bubble was a good thing.

Since Janice had left I'd felt pretty invisible when around happily hooked-up queer friends. I had started preferring to spend time with straight friends because at least then I had an identity to bounce off and they were unlikely to try to set me up with someone, anyone, to alleviate their discomfort. No, that was uncharitable. I had to stop being such a wet blanket. I knew all of my friends loved me and wanted me to be happy. Em said I needed more critical space. What I really need is a drink and a switch to turn off this gloomy internal monologue.

"Kate! Come on, I'll get you in pre-show if you like. My friend Gloria's playing." Cass spotted me and reached out a hand to move the rope, smiling at her security friend as she did so.

"I'm with Em, she's at the back. I'll have to wait with her."

"Nah, just run on up and get her and we'll go in now. Then we can start drinking sooner, eh?" Cass crushed the end of the spliff into the floor with the toe of her Docs and made a shooing gesture at me. "Go on, it's cold out here and I need a beer."

I ran back up the line to Em and found her with Grace and Kerry who, I noted, were wearing matching knitted toques, aside from a little G and a little K. I gave them each a hug and told Em the plan.

"Oh no, it's cool, I'll just wait in line with these guys and see you inside. We can't expect your friend to let us all queue-jump."

I protested but Em just laughed and shooed me away, much like Cass had done. Back at the front and there was no sign of Cass but the security guy opened the door for me and just nodded inside. I ducked under his hulking frame and smiled nervously.

There was no one on the ticket desk so I just dropped a ten onto the closed cash box and stamped my own wrist. The Biltmore was still fully illuminated as the techs set up their equipment. The harsh light revealed all the stains and scuffs normally invisible to the inebriated eye when the place was dimly lit. I spotted Cass by the stage door, talking to a woman who had her back to me. She looked familiar somehow, but out of context. I navigated the rows of chairs that had been set up in front of the stage and saw a strange smile spread across Cass's face as she noticed me approaching.

"Kate, love, you know Hanna, right?" I tried not to

11

die as all the blood rushed to my head to provide a full colour lightshow of embarrassment on my face. Fucking Cass.

"Hey." Hanna smiled at me briefly and then patted Cass on the shoulder as she nudged the stage door with her hip. "Enjoy the show. I'll catch you after, yeah?"

"Sure." Cass watched Hanna disappear and then turned to me, her eyebrows practically at her hairline. Cheeky smile perfectly in place.

I said nothing. I chewed my cheek and stood with my hands thrust into my pockets, my shoulders up near my ears.

"What!" Cass feigned innocence. "I didn't fuck her, you know. I didn't even know she'd be here. Scout's honour." She did a mock salute. Her boots clicking together. "Come on, don't be angry. Drinkies? Beer? Whisky? Both?" She put her arm around my shoulder and squeezed as we walked back to the bar.

I wanted to know what Cass and Hanna had been talking about, but it felt so juvenile to ask. Why was I even so fixated on this woman? I barely knew Hanna. It was as if Cass's insistence on my not pursuing the barista had lit some fire in me. Was Hanna a foil for some other emotion? Maybe I was just trying to avoid being single.

I looked at Cass's face, lit up by the strip lights running down the bar. She was trying to catch the barman's eye but his attention was focused on lining up glasses at the other end of the bar. He looked like a little exclamation point in his skinny black jeans and a tight black t-shirt with some tour dates on the back. He had one ear tunnelled and the back of his head shaved with a dandle of floppy curly hair on top. There was a burst of stars, just the outlines, underneath the naked ear, which struck me as a little odd. He was the perfect example of how easy it can sometimes be to confuse a hipster dyke with a cool twelve year old boy.

12

Cass pushed her hands down onto the counter and lifted herself up a notch above my head. "Hey! Hey, how's it going? My friend here needs a drink, stat!" The guy came over and smiled, his perfect teeth glowing bright in the strip lights. There was a single silver star on the front of his shirt, providing me no clue as to the band's name.

"Hey Cass, let me guess, a Deschutes porter for you and..." He looked at me inquisitively, mulling things over. I noticed that he had incredibly dark and long eyelashes. "And I bet she'll have whatever you're having, right?" He laughed and started pouring us both drinks.

"Actually, can I have a gin and tonic please? Thanks." I did actually want the porter but to hell with playing Cass's patsy for the evening.

Cass put her arm around my waist, below the bar, so her friend couldn't see. She smiled in a way that I think was supposed to be apologetic, but her face didn't seem quite able to form the right shapes. Cass never took anything seriously enough to have to apologise for it afterwards.

"Still up at UBC, Wilf?" Cass asked.

"No. I packed that shit in. Not feeling the academia these days. The band's just about done on the album and we're getting a spot on Peak later this month for the first single. Rob's plotting out some elaborate province-wide tour so I'm looking out for winter gear as it'll be freezing in that bus. We've got old coffee sacks shoved into the gaps in the floor but that's not going to cut it when we head north."

"What's the track called? I'll listen out for it if I get a chance."

"*When I Had You*," Wilf said, laughing. Cass had snorted, a little rush of her beer heading back into her glass, creating clouds of disrupted foam. "It ain't about you, you arrogant cunt. You weren't that special."

13

"Oh, but I was. I am. And you know it." Cass paid for the drinks and steered me towards the stage, taking up a spot leaning on a pillar near the stage door.

We were quiet for a moment or two and then Cass said, "Go on, just ask."

"I thought you said you'd only ever slept with women. So... Wilf and you..."

"Yeah, we hooked up in school. First-year madness. But, see, I didn't lie."

"You mean...?" I blinked.

"Well... I guess I did lie really." Cass looked momentarily confused. It didn't suit her. "I guess even back then Wilf was Wilf, he just hadn't gone through the process yet. So I guess I have slept with a guy, even if neither of us had that shit figured out. Quick, strip me of my gold star." She laughed and sipped the beer.

I was always astounded at how things just rolled off Cass. She seemed impermeable to lingering confusion. Didn't anything mean anything to her? She could quote Herodotus, write A-grade essays on othering, and then skip off to a dance party leaving a trail of empties in her wake. No wonder Hanna was interested in her. Cass had energy, oozed fun, shrugged off seriousness without a second thought, leaving dour little me in a corner still sulking over Simone and Sartre and what it all means.

Cass ran a hand through the hair falling over the side of her face and took off her glasses, clearing them of smears using the edge of her yellow and brown check shirt. As she lifted the material I saw the top of her *Rodeoh* shorts and turned away, blushing. The heat rose and fell in me, leaving my centre cold and everything else on fire.

The Biltmore was filling up fast, people forming a line at the bar while others in their party scurried to get a good table, booth, or spot near the stage. Most of the high

14

tables at the back were already taken by guests of the bands and their subdued chatter was now drowned out by the clamour of paying patrons. Kerry and Grace spotted me and waved, then pointed to the bar where Em was already in line. After a few words Grace headed our way and I introduced Cass.

"So you're the one from the dog park?! Nice to meet you. And you know the KnitWits?"

"Yeah, one of them was my Res Advisor in first year. I bumped into her again the other day at the Cobalt and, well." Cass laughed and Grace looked at me confused.

"And, well, so she's your new fuck buddy?" I asked, more for Grace's benefit than mine. I was glad that the lights had been dimmed so that my flushed face wasn't too obvious.

"Ah." Grace let out a little sigh and smiled. Her and Kerry had moved in together six months ago and were in serious nesting mode, Kerry having put her 'sleeping with the band' days behind her it seemed. I wondered if I'd ever get a chance to put such things behind me.

There was an awkward silence and I could tell that Grace desperately wanted to be in line with the others or to have a beer to swig and stare into while fiddling with the label. She was tapping the toes of her shoes together; little white oxfords that were perilously clean. I figured she planned on leaving before the dancing started, otherwise those shoes wouldn't survive the night.

"And you're in school? Cass?" Grace was trying to make conversation, but Cass's attention was focused on the stage where a woman had just appeared wearing a sheer purple dress underneath a rather odd woollen cape. This must be the KnitWits woman.

"Cass is just taking one class this semester."

"Yeah, yeah, sorry. *Applied Gender Theory in 20th Century American Literature*. I was planning on taking some others but I'm fitting them in around work so I had to push them to next semester. I don't think I'll ever finish the damned degree, but at least I've got money to pay for it!"

"And what do you do for work?"

"I edit documentaries for a non-profit. I used to make music videos but a friend hooked me up with this gig a few years back and they're really awesome people to work with so I'm happy when they call me in with extra work."

Grace gave me an odd look, quizzical somehow. I guessed she was thinking that Cass seemed an unlikely fit for charitable work. She looked back at Cass, "Isn't that tough, you know, to look at harrowing footage all day at work?"

"Nah, it's not my life, right. And it's not like there's anything I can do to help so why take it home with me." She reached into the inside pocket of her jacket and shook the little tin lightly. "Anyone for a smoke before the show starts?" She didn't wait for the response, correctly assuming that neither I nor Grace would join her outside. Grace watched her halfway across the room and then turned back to me, her eyes looking fierce. I looked away, feeling a strange protectiveness over my new friend.

"Well, she's a little odd. A bit arrogant maybe... Don't you think, Kate?"

"Yeah, I guess Cass can be a bit aloof. Nice though. Good company in the park." I realised I had said these things slowly, drawing out the blunt phrases while staring up the steps where Cass had just disappeared. I turned back to find Grace's eyebrows raised questioningly. "It's fine. She's not my type. She's too assertive and sex positive for me. You know I need someone a little less showy, a little more subtle, a bit more like..."

"Janice?" Grace offered delicately, knowing what I

16

was circling in my mind. "It's been almost a year, Kate. And as great as she was for a while she treated you like shit in the end. It's no use comparing everyone to her, however tempting."

"So I should just sleep with Cass then? And maybe half the band and the bar staff and work my way through OK Cupid until someone sticks?"

"Not a bad idea!" Kerry had arrived with drinks for her and Grace, Em puttering behind as she spilt her pint on her jacket and then spilt more as she tried to brush off the liquid before it soaked in. "So are you seeing anyone from OKC right now? Wasn't there a woman in West Van? Someone who lived in a yurt or something?"

"That was Sasha, and she lives in a cabin in Sechelt." I closed my eyes and shook my head. "Can we not talk about who I am and am not dating, just for one night, please guys?"

There was a moment or two of silence. Perhaps this was in mourning for my hopeless love life.

"Did Grace tell you?! We're getting a kitten!" Kerry kissed Grace's cheek and hi-fived Em. Did I mention that I'm a dog person?

When Cass came back, Em was still giving Kerry and Grace tips on litter box training and showing them pictures of Thunderpuss as a kitten.

"I can't deny that he's cute but until you show me a cat who can hike the Chief with you I'm sticking with dogs," Cass said and picked up her drink.

"Exactly," I said. "Or a dog that can catch a Frisbee. Although, guys, I'll totally come round to play with the kitten and cat-sit when you need, just so you know." I smiled at Grace and Kerry. They'd be good kitty-parents.

"Me too!" Em said, excitedly. "And maybe I can bring Thunderpuss over and he can teach the little one how to be extra annoying and vomit on ALL the things!"

"Thunderpuss?" Cass stopped halfway through brushing some stray ash from her scarf. Her hand hovered just below her chin and I noticed that her fingernails spooned just to the edge of her fingertips, the half-moons bright white against the pink, peppered with a few white flecks that might belie a zinc deficiency. She should smoke less and eat better, I thought. But that wasn't Cass.

"Thunderpuss is Em's cat. He's enormous because he wasn't neutered."

"They said he was neutered when I got him, but he clearly wasn't so he just kept getting bigger and bigger and then, finally, I took him to the vet. I didn't know anything about cats, not really... and he wasn't an official rescue." Em trailed off, ashamed of her slipping spot on the hierarchy of cat husbandry skills.

"He's a monster," I said, unhelpfully. "Sorry Em. But he's the biggest cat I've ever seen."

"Maybe he could catch a Frisbee?" Cass said dryly and Kerry snorted while the rest of us laughed quietly. Cass smiled at me, just a tiny smile but it was there and for a second I wondered if she was nervous about meeting my friends. Then the stage door opened again and Hanna was suddenly standing in front of us all, trying to manhandle an enormous box of t-shirts and toques and mini-EPs bearing what I assumed was her band's name: LiquorBox. Nice. She almost dropped the merchandise as one of the box's sides finally gave out, but Cass reached out a hand and held it together, artfully holding her glass aloft so as not to spill any of her beer. She gestured at me with the glass and I took it, while Cass lifted the box back up to Hanna's torso and held it until she'd regained her grip. "You got it? You OK, champ?"

"All good, thanks Cass!"

I saw that Cass's hands were over Hanna's and they

smiled at each other for a second before Hanna walked over to the merchandise table.

"Nifty ninja moves there," Kerry said to Cass.

"Thanks. I trained for seven years in -"

"Tibet?" Kerry and Cass laughed.

"More like in Coquitlam. Kids like me learnt to develop quick reflexes." Cass had told me a little about her family, how they had refused to acknowledge her when she had told them she was gay. She was twelve and they thought it just a phase, of course. They carried on letting her have sleepovers and staying at friends' places and she found that they were oddly lenient if she mentioned she was going out somewhere with a boy, so much so that she started using it as a pass to stay out late at gigs and at parties. It was almost like they figured she'd end up getting together with a guy and realise that she was into them after all. Her parents sounded more than a little misguided and, frankly, irresponsible. I think she figured that if they weren't going to protect her then she'd have to learn to do it. Who was protecting her from herself though, that's what I wondered? Teenagers don't always make the soundest of decisions after all.

Kerry started asking Cass about growing up in PoCo as she'd briefly lived there before her parents split and her dad died in a climbing accident. With a fifteen-year age gap though, they found that all their landmarks were a little off; this bar closed and that club having changed names. I figured they would probably have been pretty good friends if they'd both grown up together. They were laughing over the owner of some record store that they both knew, when Grace suddenly interrupted them.

"Kerry, sweetheart, could you get me another beer?" Grace had her hand on Kerry's elbow, having just drained her bottle of Moosehead in three large gulps.

Breaking off from her conversation with Cass,

19

Kerry looked a bit startled but readily agreed to the request. She looked at me and Em, "You guys good for drinks?"

"Fine, thanks." Em and I were slow drinkers tonight, apparently.

Cass looked at her empty glass on the side and said, "I'll come with." She started after Kerry and then reached back past me to pick up the empty, smiling at me as she turned.

"I'll come too!" Grace said and scurried after her girlfriend, slipping her arm into Kerry's as Cass led the way to the bar.

Em and I were quiet for a few seconds, then she asked, "Do you think the kitten will work? A furry Band-Aid?" She looked at me slyly over the top of her beer glass, her red lipstick oddly distorted by the amber liquid.

"Aren't they in therapy still? Or was that just a one-time thing?"

"Oh, yeah, they do that twice a month but, well, Grace was saying the other day that she's pretty sure Kerry's not done with a few of her exes, however much she protests."

"But they seem so happy. I mean, they're getting a kitten for god's sake. Who gets a kitten if they're not going to stay together?"

"Oh, yeah, right, because you haven't explained the puppy rule to me a bazillion times!" It was true, I had noted that in addition to guessing the age of a dog by the child running alongside, you could usually guess when a break-up happened by the age of the dog. Only certain breeds, usually. Mutts were harder to judge. Mutts are always more wily.

"So you really think they might break up?" I asked Em quietly.

"I hope not. I mean, they have so much going for them and they make each other really happy, when

20

they're not fighting."

"Like cats and dogs."

"Right! Did you see how annoyed Grace was just then though?" Em asked.

"But she can't think that Kerry and Cass will... well. Right? Can she? I mean they're -"

"Practically the same person," Em said, and we both laughed. "Yeah, they could be siblings, just a good few years apart. I guess Cass is reminding Grace what Kerry used to be like, and she's not too happy with that image."

I drank my G&T. "You're wasted in marketing, Em. You should be a psychotherapist." I didn't smile at her as I said this, and Em shrugged.

"It's a gift, what can I say. But, really, thinking about it, marketing is a bit like psychotherapy. I mean you have to think about your audience and what their deepest desires and fears are. Then you figure out what's stopping them achieving their dreams and conquering those fears, and then you sell your product to them in a way that makes it look like they can do both of those things really, really easily and pain-free." She got giddier as she spoke, even bouncing a little. I waited. "Of course, it's all a crock of shit and I hate it and I hate myself for doing it, but at least I have a nice apartment, and Steve and I just booked Maui for January, and I can afford to fly my sister in for a visit when she's done school. So there's that." She took a deep breath, then sighed.

"But you miss it, right? Being involved in stuff, in the community?" We both put down out drinks, serious for a moment.

"Of course. But, it's like, with Steve I don't fit any more. He gets it but… he doesn't quite get it, you know? And then, sometimes, I feel like I can't bring him with me to things, but then I want to be with him and to share stuff with him and he's just a bit oblivious or nervous, or

21

whatever." I reached out an arm and drew Em in sideways, giving her a squeeze and kissing the top of her hat.

"You're right," I said, dramatically, "it must be so tough having a big strapping guy around to help you open jars and get things on high shelves and drive you to nice hotels for the weekend, to plan babies with and to hold up the patriarchy. Sigh." I smiled at Em as she lunged at me with her little fists, pummeling my belly.

"Fuck you, you fucking queer feminist radical. Fuck you!" We scrapped until we hugged and then drank our beers in silence, turning to stare over to the bar where we could no longer see our friends. I wondered how that conversation was going.

When Cass, Grace and Kerry returned, I excused myself to use the washroom, telling Em that I'd get us drinks on the way back. I still owed Cass a beer, but that would have to wait. I'd need to grow an extra hand if I was to carry three drinks. It was fine if everyone was drinking a pint in a straight-edged glass but throw a bottle in there and I'm stumped.

As I was waiting in line for the washroom, Hanna walked up to stand behind me. LiquorBox were playing second and so she had a while to wait and didn't need to exercise band-privilege to jump the queue. We nodded at each other. "Hey."

"Hey, how's it going?"

I never knew what to do with this non-question. I always felt compelled to answer but simultaneously knew that most people didn't give a shit, so then there's this little awkward pause where you both go through the mental process of something akin to 'politeness subroutine over' and get on with the real business like asking for a book of one-zone transit tickets or ordering a coffee. The trick was to get the phrase in at exactly the

22

same time as each other and then you could both smile briefly (or not) and move to the next step of socially awkward interaction. I'd missed that opportunity here with Hanna and realised I was giving her a grim little smile instead of answering or being cool enough to have turned away. Shit.

"Great. You?" The pause had been too long and so now this just sounded weird.

"Great." Then, after another awkward pause, "Thanks."

"Excited about the show?" I asked while shuffling forward in the line, taking care to avoid the wet patch of unknown origin on the off-white tiles.

"Sure. We're debuting a new track tonight. Have you seen us before? Maybe with Cass?" Hanna smiled at me, a cool and calm expression of nonchalance on her perfect face. She had incredibly symmetrical eyebrows and nostrils. No one has symmetrical nostrils. How was that possible? Why was I staring at her nose? Why was she asking about Cass?

"First time. But I guess Cass has seen you guys before. She hasn't said, but it seems like she knows everyone somehow."

"Yeah, Cass gets around all right." Hanna smiled. What did that mean? Had Cass actually already slept with Hanna and her insistence on my not pursuing my barista crush was because she wanted her? What the fuck.

"Oh, sorry. Are you guys, like, a thing?" I guess she'd seen my face get stormy.

"No. Jeez. Friends. Just friends. Why? Are you interested in Cass? Or have you guys already, you know..." I couldn't find an appropriate way of asking what I wanted to know. She laughed and looked coy for a second.

"Maybe."

"Maybe which?" I was trying not to look too fierce

but it was hard. Then the woman behind us yelled out that there was a stall free and if I wasn't going to use it then she would. Hanna laughed again and gave me a little push on the shoulder, the flat of her hand leaving a phantom heat as I headed into the stall, not really any the wiser about whether she and Cass had hooked up.

I sat peeing as quietly as possible, listening to the conversations going on outside the stalls, trying to catch Hanna's voice. By the time I was done, Hanna had disappeared into one of the other stalls. I took a quick look in the mirror as I washed my hands, seeing the purple half-moons under my eyes, an inversion of the misguided make-up I wore as a teen. This deathly pallor was all natural though. I needed to get back into a good sleep routine, and maybe develop some kind of interest in self-accentuation. Did everyone else look this flawed underneath their make-up? Somehow, I couldn't believe that every morning before heading out to the dog park Cass stopped to apply foundation and powder and all those other accoutrements I'd failed to learn how to use properly. Still, she had brighter, smoother, clearer skin than me and she smoked and drank and partied way more than I had ever done. Maybe that was the trick. Happiness. Or maybe I was simply blind to everyone else's flaws and spent too damn long picking myself apart, I thought, turning abruptly away from the mirror and shaking my hands before wiping them on my jeans for lack of any paper towels.

At the bar, Wilf met me with a smile. It was hard to believe that this sweet-looking hipster boy had ever been involved with Cass. "Another G&T for Cass's friend and a porter for her?"

"Two porters please, thanks. Oh, and a Moosehead too." I ordered without really thinking and immediately began panicking over how I'd carry the drinks back to

24

everyone. As I was strategizing, visualising my hands, a bottle in my back pocket, or squeezed between two glasses, Hanna leant over the bar beside me.

"Hey, you ran off."

"Ah, yeah. Um, sorry?" I wasn't sure what was happening. Was I supposed to have stayed in the washroom and waited for her?

"Speedy peeing!"

"Yup, that's me. Efficiency in everything I do." What was I saying? Nonsense. Absolute nonsense, completely lacking in charm. "Can I get you a drink?" There. That was how to be cool and suave, right? Had I actually just asked her that? Who was I?

"Sure. Thanks. I'll have a double G&T. Or, well maybe a single as you're paying. I don't want to stretch your generosity."

I asked Wilf for a double. "That's cool." I thought about my dwindling bank balance and then felt like an ass for even considering it, telling myself that you have to speculate to accumulate, even in dating, perhaps. It had been an expensive summer. Fun, but a bit frivolous as I'd done a lot less hiking and a lot more drinking than in previous years. Life with Janice may have been a bit quiet but it was at least economical. Maybe that had been the problem. Maybe that's why she'd decided to travel. Without me to helpfully spend her money on everything. I imagine she's in Thailand right now, maybe sipping a cocktail from a coconut and hanging out with the locals. She always made friends much more easily when I wasn't around. Why was that? Am I that corrosive to social interaction? Would I just do the same with whoever else I got together with?

"So..." Hanna interrupted my thought spiral.

"Huh? Sorry."

"Are you OK? You kind of look exhausted. In my professional capacity as your barista I feel like you should have some coffee instead of that beer."

I laughed. Then realised she had said 'your barista.' Was Hanna mine somehow? I had been spending a lot of time in her vicinity recently, and drinking a lot of coffee. These days, I always woke up needing something strong, topping up yesterday's cold coffee concentrate with hot water to fill my travel mug for the dog park. If I didn't have my fix then I'd usually need a nap by mid-afternoon. "Maybe the problem is actually too much coffee?" I thought out loud.

"Oh, no. That can't be the case. You won't come in every day if you go cold turkey on me!"

"Maybe I should give it up for a while. I might sleep better. Starting tomorrow, no coffee for me. No caffeine even." I was determined, not really thinking the plan through but then suddenly realising what Hanna had said. If I gave it up then I'd not see her every day. Maybe that would be a good thing to give up too.

"I think this is a terrible plan," she said. I picked up the two porters and she grabbed her drink and the bottle. Problem solved. As she walked beside me back to the group she said, "Who am I going to awkwardly flirt with if you and Cass don't come in anymore?"

I looked over at her but she was a little ahead and so I couldn't read her face. Was it me or Cass she was interested in, or was she just joking?

Tentatively, I said, "Well, I would miss the flirting, so maybe I can come in for decaf."

"Phew. Sounds like a plan. I'll tell Hal to keep making those carob hockey puck things you like so much too... then you can't stay away. And, hey, there's no caffeine in carob, right?"

We got back to the group before I could reply and I handed the glass to Cass who frowned at me a little, looking pointedly over my shoulder at Hanna. She

26

murmured her thanks for the drink and set it down next to her half-empty glass. Em took the Moosehead from Hanna who then put a hand on my shoulder and told me she hoped I enjoyed the show and that she should head backstage to the band.

Once she was out of earshot, Em, Kerry and Grace all rounded on me.

"So?"

"Did you ask her out?"

"Is that your barista crush?"

I blushed, thinking that maybe there was a chance after all. "Yeah, we just talked." I sipped at my beer so as to occupy my face and hide my smile. I felt Cass's eyes on me and looked over. Was she angry at me for some reason? Was she interested in Hanna after all?

Cass got out her smokes again and raised them up, along with her eyebrows, saying "Playing with fire. It's the number one rule..." She walked off.

Kerry looked after her for a second and then turned back to me. "It's true. If she works there every day then, when things go wrong and you break up with her, you'll basically be ostracised."

"Thanks for the vote of confidence, Kerry. Why is it obviously going to go wrong?"

"Because you'll find fault with her soon enough. Then you'll try to friendzone her and then she'll try to like you but end up hating you and it'll be super awkward." She looked to Grace for back-up.

"It's true, Kate. It's kind of your pattern these days. One or two dates, some angst, and then friendzoning. I hate to say it but, well maybe Kerry's right." She smiled at her girlfriend.

"Em?" I looked over in the hope of getting some rebuttal to this character assessment. She said nothing, her eyes wide. She blinked at me a lot. Thanks Em. "Seriously guys? That's happened, like, three times since

Janice. It's not a lot."

"But that's everyone since Janice. Everyone."

"But you're the ones who are always saying that it's not been that long really and that I have to keep dating to find the right person. So, really, you're saying I have to be less picky? Is that it?"

"No!" They all cried in unison, laughing.

"Maybe just don't date this one woman," Em said, putting a hand on my arm. "I mean, unless you really think she's all that great, and there's chemistry, and you don't think you'll just get bored once you find out she doesn't like Scrabble."

"That was one time," I muttered. "One time. Seriously." Manda was cute and funny and smart but she had told me after our third date that she hated Scrabble and somehow that had been a deal breaker. I'm not even sure why. I figured it was indicative of a resistance to intellectually stimulating fun, but apparently that makes me picky. It sounded silly now these guys were pointing it out. Maybe I am too picky.

I thought about Hanna. The first time I saw her, I thought she was stunning. I figured the friendliness was professional in nature but when it carried across days and weeks I started thinking that maybe she was just naturally quite cheery, which was attractive. I had heard her talking about Jeanette Winterson once to her colleague (prompted by a restocking of the fruit bowl on the counter). She had even made a joke about never being able to get served at Kafka's and never being told why. I had had to stifle a laugh so that she didn't realise I'd been eavesdropping.

"She makes literary puns you guys. Lit-er-ary puns!"

"Well," said Grace, "how could it possibly go awry..."

They were all staring at me now and I felt interrogated. It was fine for them, all cosily domesticated.

The MC jumped on stage, saving me from further accusations about my dating record. I couldn't help glowering a little at my friends as the woman in the sheer purple dress introduced one of the support acts.

Cass wasn't back yet and I wondered if she had bumped into some people she knew and we'd lost her for the night. It was inevitable really. As the band ran through their second song, I looked around and spotted her leaning against a pillar on the other side of the room.

Her body was pointed at the stage but she was looking at me, her arms folded and her legs crossed at the ankle. It was at once a pose of stillness and intense aggravation. She looked away quickly and then I watched as some girl in a tea dress and military boots bounced up behind her and handed her a bottle of Kokanee. Cass hated Kokanee. She immediately started peeling at the blue label, nodding thanks at the girl who was leaning into her and talking non-stop. Cass looked up at me again and now it was my turn to look away. I concentrated on the band for the next couple of songs and when I looked back Cass and the girl were gone. I picked up the beer I had bought for her and cradled it until the band's set was done and LiquorBox started moving things around on stage.

Em and Grace were talking about the mediocrity of the first band. None of us had heard of them before and the lead singer had a whiny voice and a floppy coiffure that kept reflecting the stage lights in a greasy glare. Their final song appeared to be some awful reflection on a relationship with someone who too closely resembled the lyricist's mother. I hoped she wasn't in the audience.

"Isn't it odd how often hipster boy bands have vaguely misogynistic lyrics?" I said to Kerry, who was staring intently at her iPhone and didn't reply. Unless I appended a name to every sentence this was often the way things went with friends. It's similar to puppy training, where you quickly realise that your dog's name serves as a marker for them to listen to you amidst the general drivel pouring forth from your mouth each day. Don't say, "Sit, Rover," and then get annoyed as your dog stares at you expectantly. It's not their fault you haven't figured it out. Same with the iPhone.

"Kerry, isn't it odd that hipster boy bands -" Grace cut me off as she thrust her own iPhone under Kerry's nose.

"Look! Squee! VOKRA just sent us an email!"

I drank my beer while they read about their potential new foster kitten and bounced up and down. I resisted the urge to get out my own phone as I knew it would likely lead to some slightly tipsy texting of someone I didn't even really want to talk to. Probably one of those women who'd disappointed me in not liking Scrabble. I contented myself with watching Hanna set up her drums on stage. There really was little doubt now about her queerness.

Em saw me watching Hanna and whispered in my ear "If you like her that much then, fuck it, just ask her out."

I looked over my shoulder at her. "Really? What about the not-banging-the-barista rule that you guys all think is so essential?"

"There are other coffee shops and, who knows, maybe she plays Scrabble in addition to being hot and making lit-er-ary jokes. At least you'll get good coffee every morning for a while." I thought about waking up next to Hanna and immediately started panicking about the night before. Even after five years with Janice, and a couple of flings this year, the thought of actively engaging in sex was terrifying. What if she found my stretch marks grotesque or realised that I have dry skin on the inside of my elbow, or what if I squashed her or accidentally poked her in the face?

30

"I don't even know if she's queer," I said, trying to give myself an out now I was actually getting some friendly support for my crush.

"She's in a band called LiquorBox," Em said, frowning at me disapprovingly.

"So? That doesn't necessarily mean everyone in the band is queer."

"She's the drummer in a band called LiquorBox." She paused, pointedly. "You're just being wilfully obtuse. Stop it. Go ask her out. Properly this time." I recalled how I'd stammered to the point of requesting a pen last time I'd tried and, oddly enough, this didn't help quell the rising anxiety.

"She's on stage, Em. People like me do not climb onto a stage in front of a room full of people and ask out hot drummers."

"Maybe that's why you don't date hot drummers." She took hold of my drink and gave me a little shove towards the stage.

Hanna was still alone, concentrating on moving things around. She looked so assured, so comfortable. I felt like throwing up. I realised now why it was that she had such amazing arms, shown off to perfection in the cut off t-shirts she often wore at the coffee shop. Oddly, she didn't seem to have any tattoos. I tried to recall ever having seen more than just her arms and shoulders though and couldn't. Maybe her whole torso was covered in them and she just hid them at work. Em nudged me in the back again. "Go!"

I swallowed and started over to the stage, then turned around and fished out the bottle of water from my bag. I'd just go over and tell her I knew drumming was sweaty work. That would be fine, right? Or, was that too gross? Would she think I was disgusted by her? But if I wanted to keep her hydrated then she'd know I cared. Right? Em was looking at me with a disappointed face. I took a breath and steeled myself to stride up to the stage, but when I looked up again I saw Hanna leaning down to take a bottle of beer from Cass, the two of them laughing. Then Hanna ruffled Cass's hair and went back to setting things up.

"Ouch." Em handed me my drink again and put an arm over my shoulder to spin me back to face everyone. "Maybe wait for that little sex-fest to be over before you have a go, eh?"

"I think I might go home you guys." I felt perilously close to tears, which was stupid as I didn't even know Hanna and couldn't be that hung up on her. Why did Cass have to hone in on her though and be so fucking cool about it all? Wasn't she just accepting drinks from the tea-dress girl anyway?

"Sweetie, just stay. You'll get to see your favourite drummer perform, and then KnitWits are on after, and they're so good. You can't just go home to sulk. You'll be unhappier there and you know it. Why let Cass ruin your night?"

"What happened?" Grace looked back and forth at me and Em, her phone still nestling in her hands, ready to draw her back in at any moment.

"Cass is stealing the sexy drummer, just as Kate was about to go and make her move."

"Oh, the barista is the drummer? Didn't you decide not to go there anyway?"

"No. You all decided I shouldn't and in the meantime Cass decided Hanna was fair game and so now I've missed my opportunity and lost a potential girlfriend and possibly a friend."

"But why be friends with someone who is so blatantly trying to hook up with your crush? It's a bit of a dick move. Cass seems like a player. You shouldn't be taking dating lessons from her," Grace said and then looked at Kerry, almost as if she were about to apologise.

Kerry looked back at her, not quite sure if she should take offence.

"What? You think that I used to do that? Fuck friends over for girls?" She adopted a scary voice and waved her hands as she said, "In my bad old days."

Em and I both started chewing on our upper lips.

"No," Grace said. "I just, well. Just that you were talking to Cass earlier and it seemed like you had lots in common and so..." Grace trailed off and we were all silent for a few seconds.

"So, this cat?" I said, trying to be helpful. "What's the deal guys? Is there a pussy party happening at yours this weekend or what?" Em laughed but Kerry and Grace were keeping their faces as still as they could. I buried my face in my beer and tried not to look at the stage, at Hanna, and her arms. Cass had disappeared again but I wasn't about to try to track her down. Fuck her. Clearly she'd just been warning me off Hanna so that she could get in there. Now I didn't stand a chance, not against Cass and all her mystique and allure and plaid and sexy ruffled hair.

CHAPTER FOUR

I awoke from a nightmare about drowning, my limbs
paralysed by fear, only to find that I was actually just
completely tangled in damp, sweaty sheets. I prised my
mouth apart with a dry smacking sound, and became
aware of how my brain felt like a dried-up back-of-the-
cupboard raisin in a loud cavernous skull. I did not
remember getting home. I groaned and rolled to the edge
of my bed to sprawl out my limbs. I felt hot breath on
my face and opened my eyes to see my dog, Jupiter,
bright-eyed and waggy-of-tail. I groaned again and Jupiter
actually recoiled from my stinky breath. This was a new
low.

"Jupiter, take yourself for a walk. I do not exist
today." He heard the word 'walk' and ran off to fetch his
lead. Damn dog and his lack of contextual
understanding. He stood in the doorway to my bedroom,
his lead in his mouth, his tail pounding against the door
like an evil percussive brain worm. As I stared at him,
unmoving, his tail wags grew less enthusiastic and then
stopped, his tail dropping slowly back down like a

barometer of expected fun. I felt like a terrible person, but I was not yet capable of moving. I had to process last night first.

I remembered seeing Hanna on stage, drumming with LiquorBox. She was good. Really good. Then there had been another round of drinks. I remembered seeing Cass talking to Wilf at the bar and then, I think, no. Wait, had I ended up outside with Cass? I didn't remember. I did remember Grace and Kerry leaving, not speaking to each other, and then Em must have helped me home because I was somehow here, undressed, in my own bed, with a glass of water on the bedside table and, oh thank god, a couple of Tylenol. I owed Em a drink. No. A coffee. No, hadn't I decided to quit drinking coffee? I owed Em a hug, after I'd showered and brushed my teeth with all the toothpaste in the world.

I swallowed the Tylenol, wary of opening up a passage from my stomach to my oesophagus in case the contents of the former formed designs on escaping the latter. Close quickly pyloric valve, I thought.

Switching to morning dog-routine autopilot I pulled on whatever clothes were nearest, grabbed the park bag with an already filled water bottle and left the apartment with Jupiter. Had I even walked him last night? It had been so long since I'd been this hung over, or even that drunk, not since I'd had Jupiter to look after. I gave him an ear scritch and a lopsided smile and then kissed his head and asked him to forgive me. I knew he had already, dogs are good like that.

His bladder needs clearly weren't that urgent so I figured Em must have taken him out after escorting me home. I owed her big-time. Jupiter loves Em so was probably super happy for a midnight walk, or two am walk, or whenever it was that we got in. Walking through Robson Park, I suddenly realised that I might bump into Cass if she was walking Hobbes. I blinked, trying to clear the blear from my eyes, and scanned the park. No sign of her or the noisy little scruffball that liked to leap at Jupiter. My amiable pooch had spent many an hour peering down at Hobbes from a great height, wondering what all the ruckus was about. I was glad both not to have the yip of the little dog reverberating in my brain and also not to have to talk to Cass. I was still pissed off about Hanna, and if I hadn't felt so awful I may have walked down to the café to see if the lovely barista was working today. Jupiter can be a pretty great flirt when he wants. I realised that I probably looked super rough though. Another good reason not to run into Cass. So after walking down to the Drive and back, Jupiter and I crawled into bed with some tea and a giant bag of Veggie Sticks. I let him have a few; just the green ones, figuring they were healthy, perhaps.

I sent Em a text to say thanks for last night, and Jupiter and I watched *Degrassi* for an hour or so. I knew I should get up and do some work but I didn't have to be in the office today so it was easy enough to convince myself it was the weekend. Jupiter seemed happy to use me as a pillow and once he's upside down and snoring there's really no way that I can move. I'm trapped beneath the adorable giant beast. More *Degrassi*.

This time when I woke up it was because Jupiter was licking my face. He wasn't intending to, it was just that his paws were on my pillow and his aim's not great. Barely escaping with my eyeball, I reached for my phone. It was already two in the afternoon and I'd done nothing productive. It would soon be going dark so I almost felt like the day was a write-off anyway, but, with it being near the end of the month, I had to tie up some projects. The thought of going into work tomorrow with nothing to show for today was arguably more painful than my head, and my hip. Why was my hip hurting? I shuffled

36

Jupiter out of the way and took a look, seeing the impressive bruise blooming on my outer thigh. Jupiter stared at me, aghast, while I grimaced and realised that I must have fallen on my ass at some point last night. Classy.

I decided to give up alcohol and coffee, and women. "Jupiter, it's just you and me." He yawned. I'm not sure he likes that plan. Clearly I'm not enough for him. "Biscuits?" That got his attention. We went to the kitchen and shared some carob drops. Two for me, one for him. I balanced a row of five on his nose and made him wait for a second then said, "Go!" Jupiter fired carob drops all over the kitchen. Probably not my finest idea. At least it kept him entertained while I made him some proper food.

As I opened the refrigerator, I noticed that the magnets had been moved around. I must've knocked them last night and Em had obviously rearranged them. My phone vibrated in my pocket. It was a message from Cass asking "How ya feelin, champ?" I put my phone back in my pocket without replying. Her hangover was probably worse than mine, knowing her usual style. I wondered if she'd gone home with Hanna last night.

Jupiter had found all the carob drops and was staring dolefully at me as I stared dolefully into the bright light of the refrigerator. There were so many things and yet nothing seemed to fit together today. I looked back at Jupiter. "Pizza?" He cocked his head to the left. "Uncle Fatih's?" He wagged his tail in that optimistic way dogs do. "Uncle Fatih's it is." Sometimes it was nice to have a friend to bounce ideas off.

By the time the pizza arrived, I had showered and made myself feel a little more human. I was even sitting at my desk and answering emails in a semi-cogent fashion. It felt like I had matured ten years in the last twenty minutes. I transferred three slices of pizza to a baking tray and threw on a handful of Daiya before putting it under the grill for a couple of minutes. That way the toppings wouldn't all fall off; the peril of many a cheeseless pizza. I stuck a wedge of crust in Jupiter's bowl, along with his peppers and pineapple chunks.

He had fallen asleep again and so I took the bowl over to him and he languidly reached out his huge tongue to see what was in there without even moving his head. Seriously. This dog has it all figured out.

I worked until nine and then took Jupiter out with his flashing ball. Some teenagers were smoking weed on the benches at the side of the park and I imagined it must have been quite weird watching this seemingly autonomous pink glowing ball bouncing around and then illuminating the mouth of a giant black dog. It was at least five years since I'd gotten high, and it hadn't been fun, not like when I was a teenager. I guess I had gotten more paranoid in my twenties, more concerned with making a good impression, keeping my cool. It was also a long time since I'd been as drunk as last night.

It was strange that Hanna had me so upset that I'd just downed beer after beer. Maybe it wasn't her at all, but the slipping of my life into my thirties with no partner, no career progression, no house, no funding in place for the movie Janice and I had planned on making. Would dating Hanna really solve any of that? Had I become constitutionally incapable of having fun for the sake of fun? Did everything have to have an endgame? Maybe that was the real reason I'd drowned my brain last night and probably made a tit of myself in the process. Beer-shaped release valves are always a bad plan.

Jupiter had slumped at my feet, the ball perfectly positioned between his front paws. He looked up at me expectantly and I filled up the little water bowl I always brought to the park. I bobbed down beside him and stroked his ears for a while, staring into the darkness and then glancing up at the lights on Grouse Mountain. Cass had mentioned doing a hike with the dogs sometime soon. I should just swallow my pride, I thought, and be happy if Cass and Hanna have some fun. I don't own either of them, after all. "Right Jupes?" He gulped and carried on panting. "Let's just talk to Cass in the morning and pretend like nothing happened and everything's cool, yes? Do you think you can do that?" The big brown eyes were sceptical but I was resolute. "You and Hobbes and Cass and I will all go hiking and she can even bring Hanna if she wants. Right?" No response. "It'll be fine," I said, more to myself this time, "it'll be fine."

We didn't see Cass the next day though. She had probably gone running with Hobbes or headed to a park closer to her work. Jupiter and I shuffled around Robson, uninspired, ill at ease in case the dogcatchers descended. When it was this rainy and grim no one but dogs and the people they own are going to be in the park though. There should be a new sub clause for rain in the by-laws. I'd get right on amending city regulations when I got home. That, and focusing on my career.

Cass wasn't at the park the next day either, and I realised that I'd never responded to her text. Maybe she'd taken offence and now wasn't talking to me. I suddenly felt like I was twelve again as I stood in the Vancouver drizzle and contemplated having no friends and being the un-fun one who was just sad and got drunk and fell over and had to be helped to bed. I wasn't fit to have a dog to look after, although Jupiter seemed pretty pleased that my reclusive status had continued for two days and he'd had me all to himself. If I could just meet someone like Jupiter... That's a terrible train of thought. I clipped on his leash and we splashed home through the sunken puddle-riddled sidewalks, full of fall's golden browns and yellows.

I wondered where Cass was. Perhaps she was hanging out at Matchstick, writing in her little black notebook, a Cowichan sweater keeping her warm over a prim, but unironed button-down. We had met there for our first 'friend-date,' Cass bringing her Scrabble board and me keeping score because, as it turned out, she was hopeless at math. We had decided to give ourselves double points for flirty words due to the plethora of hot queers who kept sauntering into the coffee shop in various states of asymmetry. Alas, Cass started off play with 'kale' and I followed with 'karma.' If 'kale' had been my word I'd have argued it was flirty. I mean, really, what better way to seduce a vegan in Vancouver, right? Drop in a little nutritional yeast and you may as well be getting married already.

Scrabble, it turned out, was the perfect friend-date activity with Cass. We were relaxed enough to take long slow turns, and pepper those words we did put down with conversation. This was mainly about school, our exes, writing and good coffee shops in which to hang out. This is when Cass had introduced me to the barista rule. It made sense. Maybe it made more sense for her though, as she was liable to work her way through the entire staff at a coffee shop, leaving them all wanting more and then hating her and each other.

As we reached the heights of Scrabble desperation, Cass had headed outside for a smoke and I watched her pacing, fully expecting her to get out her iPhone like my other friends always did when there was any possibility of thought unfiltered by social media. Instead, she had opened up the little black notebook that had been tucked inside her jacket pocket, the pencil attached to it by a ratty piece of string, and she'd let her cigarette die on her lips as she scribbled furiously. I had looked back down at

40

my letters and tried to find a place on the board to put a wayward 'Q.' When I had looked back up it seemed like Cass was staring at me through the window but she quickly looked down again and folded the notebook back into her pocket, putting the half-smoked cigarette back into her tin. In the growing gloom of the Vancouver afternoon, she raised her face to the sky for a second, her hair falling backwards as she took a deep breath of damp air. With the mock army boots, skinny jeans, shirt, sweater, and leather jacket combo, topped by the tortoiseshell glasses it was as if she had jumped from a page in an East Van fashion catalogue, but at the same time I remember thinking that she was so very essentially Cass.

Now I was walking back from the park and wondering where my friend had gone. I missed her and Hobbes. While Jupiter and I had fun in the park every morning it was always nice to have Cass there for a Seneca-like premeditation on the day, and to catch up on the antics of her evening. There was something so honest about our interactions. At first I had figured it was simply because we only ever saw each other in the park. Later, I realised that Cass was often just brutally honest about life as a way of defending herself against disappointment.

When we first met, nothing I said felt weighed down by expectations built up in the context of mutual friendships. After a while, I felt like Cass had let her guard down, seeing that I, too, was unencumbered by her history. If anything it seemed that being slightly removed from each other's worlds meant we could be almost objective, or at least provide a perspective unlike anyone else. She called me out on shit that I didn't think any of my other friends would. Perhaps that was just a product of the situation though, rather than a vital quality of our interactions. I guess it might change now that we'd started hanging out away from the dog park and for a second or two I almost regretted making that leap. Almost.

CHAPTER FIVE

Em was standing outside my apartment when Jupiter and I got back. Her hand was poised over the intercom, but dropped as she saw us walking up.

"Oh, hey," Em said, "I texted. Did you not get it?" I retrieved my phone from my soggy pocket and saw three new messages, two from Em, and one from Cass.

"Sorry. I guess I didn't hear over the sound of incessant rain pounding on my skull." I went to give Em a hug and then we both backed off and scowled. "Sorry, soggy." Jupiter got between us and shook himself seventy-percent dryer. Luckily Em was the kind of friend who laughed at such things, wiping the mud spatter from the front of her coat.

"Coffee?" she said.

"Here or out?"

"At Our Town? Or is that too awkward?"

I concentrated on towelling off Jupiter and wondered what Cass's message said. It might be about Hanna. Maybe she hadn't been in the park because the two of them had been in bed for two days straight.

43

Maybe she'd finally come up for air. Maybe they'd be at the café and we could accidentally run into them.

"Sure. Let's go there. It's fine," I said, and Em smiled at me and held the door open. I put some fresh water down for Jupiter and kissed his forehead. "Be good. Don't eBay."

"He's such a devil for that, eh?" Em said.

As we walked back down the stairs, I checked Cass's message: "Hey, how's it going? Missed you yesterday. Coming to the park soon? Maybe Lynn Valley loop tomorrow?" She must've just left the park as we'd arrived this morning. I imagined her standing in her big green coat, faux fur hood all up around her ears, in danger of catching fire with her morning spliff, her fingers freezing as she texted. No mention of Hanna, which was interesting. Em had said something but I missed it.

"What? Sorry. Texts."

"I said that you didn't need to thank me for the other night. All I did was call a cab for you and Cass."

"Huh? What was Cass doing?" My brain was trying to rewind but it seemed that the mental footage of that night had been dipped in absinthe and set on fire.

"Er... she was helping you get home." Em looked at me puzzled. "You totally don't remember do you? Wow. I didn't realise you were that drunk."

"And my bruise?" My hip had turned a horrific shade of purple.

"What bruise?"

"I must've fallen over and made a fool of myself. But you... you didn't see? And, what, I got a cab with Cass?"

"She took you home I guess. Maybe she realised how drunk you were. I was a bit tipsy. I even went home and tried to wake Steve up to fuck me. Oh, shit. You and Cass didn't... you know? Hook up..." Em had actually clamped her hand over her mouth and we stood for a

44

second outside the café. Suddenly it seemed like a really bad idea to be there.

"I honestly have no idea. Someone put me to bed, possibly undressed me, left me two Tylenol and a glass of water, walked Jupiter and rearranged my fridge magnets."

"Your fridge magnets?"

"Weird, right?"

"But, your fridge magnets are all in the shape of a heart right now."

"No they're not."

"Yes. Yes they are. I just saw them!" Em got her phone out and started scrolling. She thrust it into my face. "Look! I Instagrammed it because I thought it was cute."

She was right. The magnets did form a sort of heart shape. I stared at Em. What did this mean?

"So. Let me get this straight," Em said. "Cass made sure you got home safe, left you with medical provisions for the stonking hangover you were going to have, clearly watched you fall on your ass at some point, possibly saw you naked, and then left you a heart-shaped message on your refrigerator door. Yeah. That's not saying something."

I was dumbfounded.

"I knew it," Em said. "I damn well knew it. She likes you!"

"No. She's way too cool." It couldn't be true. I felt my face getting hot.

"Oh shit!" Em was bouncing up and down. "And you like her! Look at you! You're bright red. Fuck!"

"Em, shut up. Cass is just a friend and anyway she was trying to hook up with Hanna." None of this seemed to make sense any more.

"And did she hook up with Hanna?" Em said sagely.

"Well, no I don't think so."

45

"And did she see you naked and leave you a heart-felt message?" Em was grinning in a very annoying way.

"Maybe," I muttered. "Shall we go somewhere else for coffee?" I looked into the café but couldn't see if Hanna was there or not.

"No. We're here. Maybe we can ask Hanna if she's seen Cass!" Em was enjoying this way too much.

"Fine," I said as we walked in and scanned the place for seats, spotting a free table by the wall of movie star photos.

Em went to get us drinks, treating me to a decaf latte despite the disapproving look she'd given me when I'd said the 'd' word. One thing I was sure of was the need to decrease my coffee and alcohol intake. It was clearly doing odd things to my brain and my gut was already churning with the idea that Cass might like me. Sure, she'd helped me home, put me to bed, appreciated, as one dog owner to another, that Jupiter needed looking after, and then she'd decided to fuck with me by messing up the magnets. She was probably waiting for me to say something about them, to risk bringing things up so she could mock me for thinking she liked me. That must be it.

"She's just fucking with me, that's all," I said as I saw Em approach with her coffee.

"Who's fucking with you?" I looked up and saw Hanna standing just behind Em, my latte in her outstretched hand.

I didn't say anything, just smiled wanly, already embarrassed.

"Cass," Em said, turning to Hanna. I shot her a warning look but she had obviously decided to ignore me and focus on my barista crush.

Hanna looked at me in what I thought was a disappointed way, but it was hard to tell. Her face was almost always cheerful and I had not yet developed a gauge for her less happy expressions.

"Why is Cass fucking with you? Is everything all right? Did something happen to you last night?" She peered at me curiously and I wondered how awful I looked, my hung over body not able to bounce back as it had done in my early twenties. Time to grow up I guess.

"Em is just joking. It's fine. I just got a bit drunk last night it seems." I had the sudden horrible thought that Hanna had accompanied us in the taxi, had witnessed me falling on my ass or drooling or, oh god, throwing up or getting naked. I apologised in case any of the above had happened but Hanna just smiled, amused.

"I saw nothing but impeccable behaviour. You even bought me a drink, so don't worry we're definitely still friends." She put an odd emphasis on the last word and I had to look away as she continued staring at me.
Em was pulling up an extra seat and gestured for Hanna to join us but she declined.

"Sorry, I should get back to the counter. Break's over." She bit her lower lip for a second and then cocked her head slightly to one side. "Would you, er, are you maybe free tomorrow night? There's a poetry slam going on and I thought I might have heard you say you were into that kind of thing so would you maybe -"

"She'd love to." Em jumped in, kicking my leg under the table and causing me to grunt in a less than suave fashion.

"Urgh. Ahem. Uh huh. That'd be great. I do try to go to the slams whenever I can."

"Awesome. I get off work at five so I could meet you on the Drive at 6ish if you wanted to get a drink and some food first?"

"Sure."

"Well, just text or call if you have to cancel or anything." Hanna handed me a napkin with her number scrawled in black ink. "Otherwise, see you there."

47

"Awesome. Er, great." She smiled and then returned to the counter. I had said awesome, I never say awesome. When had I become a person who says awesome? When hot women ask me out, I guess.

Em was peering at me over her coffee mug. I met her eyes and she started shaking with the effort of not laughing out loud.

"Shut up."

She gave me a 'what?' look. "Seriously. Shut up."

"OK OK. I can't stand it." She laughed. "So Cass is in love with you - "

"Woah!"

"And then your hot barista asks you out. Maybe I should start getting royally drunk. Seems to work pretty well for you!"

"Cass is not in love with me. And, well, I'm as surprised as you that Hanna is interested. I thought she liked Cass."

"Well, maybe the three of you can have a hot little tryst. She probably has great coordination and arm strength, what with all that drumming and coffee making. Cass on one fist, you on the other."

"You're vile and disgusting."

"Hey, you're the one with all the chicks after you."

"Em? Chicks? Really?"

"Charmer." She grinned.

"Shut up."

"Cad."

"Shut - "

"Player."

"Em!"

She was laughing uncontrollably and it was contagious. Every sucked in breath made my belly hurt though, so I made a concerted effort to calm down, looking away from Em so her face didn't set me off again.

Serious for a second, I said, "Maybe I should text Cass and tell her about my date with Hanna." Em laughed even harder but the thought of talking to Cass had sobered me up. What if she did actually like me? What if the real reason she had been trying to stop me from seeing Hanna wasn't because I'd get us ostracised from the café but because she was jealous?

CHAPTER SIX

It started to drizzle as I pounded down Broadway towards the Drive. My face was being pelted with rain and I thought longingly about my sofa where, just minutes before, I'd left Jupiter curled up on top of Em. She had volunteered to Jupiter-sit for the night so that I didn't have to worry about cutting short my date with Hanna. I think she was also glad to have some time away from Steve. They seemed happy for the most part but Em was pretty good at recognising when a relationship needed some space, whereas Steve was a smotherer through and through, fixing every problem with more sex, assuming that the bliss he felt after he came would last forever and solve everything.

It's funny what people's minds turn to after orgasm. I had always marvelled at how Janice would start talking about school, gossip, a *TED talk* she'd seen or some other random shit after I flopped down next to her, elbows aching from propping myself upright between her thighs. My mind always took a while to put itself back together after I came. There'd be too many colours for

50

my brain to hold onto, too much noise pinging and whooshing inside my skull. I just wanted silence, to get myself back to myself before reality set back in. Janice would compartmentalise sex. Once it was done it was done, why bother enjoying the lingering pattern of our heavy breathing, the racing heartbeat. I had hated that. It felt perfunctory, meaningless. It gave everything an air of ridiculousness, more so than sex already had in all its squelching and oozing and sucking.

Had it really been almost a year since I had last slipped into bed beside Janice? Her body already as far over to her side as could be, nothing visible above the sheets aside from the shiny mess of dark curls fanned out onto her pillow. Jupiter used to crawl up in between us and at first we had laughed at this, shooing him off the bed as we clutched at each other, working at exploring our bodies together, wrapping limbs over and under, gasping at the sudden delight of discovering the other's arousal. Janice's body was incredible. She had these strong, limber legs that would wrap around me, pinning me to her, but all the while staying soft, responsive to the gentlest of caresses. I had loved to brush my lips over her collarbone, use my tongue to pull her hardened nipples in between my teeth, to tease a little groan of pleasure as I slid my fingers inside her.

When had it all fallen apart? I hadn't noticed things changing, but then, suddenly, everything had been different. The tiniest little things would sink her into a week-long gloom and I could do nothing to lift her out of it. The more I had tried the more I realised that my not being able to help actually made it worse. She should have been able to rely on me and I just kept failing her. Some days it was like I was barely even there, not registering as a distinct entity, as part of her world. She would work around me, picking up books I'd left lying on the counter, the dining table, the couch, returning

51

them to the shelves even if there was a bookmark halfway through. I began to feel like an unwanted child, someone she had a responsibility for but who was holding her back from being so much more than simply someone who loved me. I had watched myself become less and less important to her and, in turn, I could do less and less to help bring her back to happiness.

I stood at the intersection, watching the people pour out of the Skytrain station and onto the B-Line. I used my wristwarmer to brush away the tear that threatened to release a flood. This was some pre-date pep talk I was giving myself. Standing on the street crying wasn't a great start to a date with the woman I'd been idolising for months. Maybe I wasn't ready for this yet. Maybe I still had too much of myself tied up in Janice to give all of me to someone else. Maybe, though, I needed to chill the fuck out and not treat this date like it was the beginning of a steady process to marriage and kids and the happy ever after. It was just a date, with the hot barista I'd been mooning over all summer. So, if I was so into her, why did I just feel like turning around and going home?

My phone buzzed in my jacket pocket and I peered down at the message as I weaved through the oncoming people crossing the street. "I hear you've got a hot frothy date with a certain barista. Let me know how it goes?" Cass. How was it that she always knew everything? Maybe I should've told her earlier, before she found out from someone else. Anyway, it didn't seem like she was really all that bothered. She wouldn't have texted if she was jealous, right?

CHAPTER SEVEN

Although I couldn't hear the sucking, sticky sounds of my shoes in the beer soaked floor I knew that they were there, beneath the layers of bass pounding into my skull. I worried that if I stood still for too long I'd have to leave my shoes behind, be carried hand over hand to the entrance and run home barefoot. Hanna turned and handed me a bottle, clinking hers to mine and then taking a swig. She yelled something at me but I couldn't work out the words. I looked at her quizzically and she took my hand in hers, wrapping her arm around my waist and moving us in a little dance.

"Sure!" I yelled at her, nodding in what I hoped was an inspiring fashion. Everything would be fine if we just got on the dance floor and lost our inhibitions.

Since we'd entered the Cobalt, I hadn't recognised any of the songs, which didn't surprise me too much as the usual fare here rarely included anything I loved. Normally, though, I could at least make out distinct songs, but tonight it seemed like a continuous dirge of samples remixed to death. Hanna, however, was making an effort to dance, so it was only fair that I tried. A wave of tiredness hit me again and I thought eagerly of crawling into bed, alone. It was only Monday and I felt like it had been an exhausting week already. How was I supposed to meet someone if I just felt old and tired and reclusive all the time? Until someone invented speed-dating at my house, while I was in my pyjamas with a cup of tea and Jupiter lying on my feet, I seemed destined to be alone forever.

Hanna put both her hands around my waist, pulling me both closer and back into the present moment. She pushed her thigh between my legs and I responded in kind, stiffening my leg and using my free hand to cup her ass so as to control the grind. She slipped a hand up to the back of my head, her fingers grasping at my hair, as she lowered her eyes in sultry concentration. I was starting to warm up a little. She was, after all, very, very sexy. She flickered her eyes up to mine and then kissed me, our rhythmic slow grind almost stopping entirely. Her top lip brushed over mine and her tongue darted in to reach my tongue. Then she dared a few little biting forays, getting a measure of my playfulness, testing and teasing, bolder with each riposte. She adjusted her body a little, moving her head alongside mine, breaking the kiss so she could drag her tongue underneath my ear lobe, giving me a little nibble for good measure. We stayed locked like this for a few seconds and I opened my eyes, the sweaty heaving dancers still there outside the silence of our small embrace.

Someone knocked into us from behind and we broke apart, in danger of falling unless we steadied ourselves separately. Hanna laughed and resumed dancing, but I scanned the throng, trying to figure out who had interrupted us. No one had been that close to us. It was probably just an accident but, for whatever reason, it had felt deliberate. I took a sip of my beer and reached out for Hanna's hand, pulling her back into me, determined to be a bit more engaged, a tad more suave. When the next track came on Hanna gestured in the direction of the washroom. I nodded, tapped my beer, and pointed at the bar. She smiled and then gave me a brief, exuberant kiss before bouncing off the dance floor.

At the bar I made the mistake of leaning on my elbows, trying to gain a little height so the server would notice me. As I wiped the beer off my arms onto my jeans someone tapped me on the shoulder. I turned, expecting to see Hanna. Cass was standing just inches away from me, grinning. Her eyes were fierce; pupils narrowed almost to the point of invisibility. She looked like a superhero. A crazy superhero about to kick the shit out of some bad guy, maybe. Or, perhaps she was a supervillain. I couldn't trust myself to tell the difference anymore.

Cass said something, but I couldn't make out the words. I tapped my ear and shrugged. She yelled something again but I just shook my head. Grabbing my elbow, she turned me around and started frogmarching me towards a quieter corner. Her breath curled around my ear, making me shudder as she said, "Let's go talk." We stumbled over to the wall, slotting neatly into a gap near the pinball machine. She still had hold of my wrist as I stood, back to the wall, looking up at her, into those insanely green eyes.

"Cass? Are you OK?" I was starting to worry. I'd never seen her when she was so high before, usually just seeing the aftermath in the park the next day, her brain a little slower to form witty one-liners. She was grinning. Her lips, usually so soft and pink, were stretched and pale against her teeth. I could smell the cigarettes on her breath and felt an urge to turn my head away but then she pushed herself against me and kissed me, her teeth banging into mine, my lips squashed painfully as my head jammed up against the wall. This was not how it was supposed to happen. Why had she ruined it? Why had I just realised how badly I wanted her and how wrong we would be for each other?

I used my free hand to grip a chunk of her jacket and pull her away, then thrust my other hand against her belly and pushed us apart. I fought the urge to pull her back into me but it just wasn't right, not like this. I clenched my jaw and stared at her, my breath hurting my lungs as I pulled in air. She stood and stared at me, her arms dangling uselessly by her sides, her face blank, impassive. It was as if she had just turned herself off, no longer registering the world outside herself. Then she swallowed and blinked and met my eyes for the briefest moment before heading towards the exit.

I remained standing up against the wall, my back flat to the sweaty paint and plaster. I was still gaping in shock and I realised that, beside me, a group of women were barely able to constrain their laughter. I shook myself free of the wall and closed my mouth, imaging that these women were thinking I was some baby-dyke or straight interloper who Cass was giving a taste, scaring me out of the idea that all women are soft and gentle and unthreatening. What the fuck was Cass thinking? Had she seen me with Hanna? I suddenly had a sick feeling that she was the one who had knocked into us, with purpose.

I wanted to go home and crawl into bed and never leave. I had to find Hanna though. Clearly, I couldn't just leave, even though I was suddenly desperate for air, for the blackness of the night, the rush of cold rain on my skin. I'd just tell Hanna I was coming down with something, or that Em had called and said Jupiter was sick.

I walked around the Cobalt but I couldn't find Hanna anywhere. I checked to see if she'd waited at either bar for me but there was no sign of her. I checked the washrooms and then went outside, making sure I'd not gotten any messages or calls. There was nothing, no word from her. I sent a quick text to ask where she was and waited in the rain, listening to the traffic rolling through the surface water. Some women stumbled out of the club and a couple of the security guys took up positions to block their re-entry, arms firmly folded, taking no bullshit. The women yelled at the guards to go fuck themselves and I peered cautiously out from under my hat, trying to detect even the slightest twitch in an eyebrow or a lip to betray a lack of inner calm or professionalism, maybe a soupçon of amusement. There was nothing. The women moved on, clearly seeing that they weren't going to get a rise from these guys.

There was no sign of Hanna. I sent another text saying that I'd wait another few minutes, that maybe she'd gone home already and could she let me know. The rain was heavier now and my hat, my head, became soaked, the water running down into my eyes. I wished I'd not bothered scratching eyeliner onto my lids earlier. It was going to start stinging soon so I used a tissue from my pocket to dry my face, hoping to avoid garish black smears of unfortunate make-up. A cab went by, close to the kerb, and a whoosh of water splashed up against my legs, the rainbow mix of oil and rain dripping down my jeans. I shook my legs one at a time and then set off at a quick march home, hoping that the walk would clear my head.

By the time I arrived home my eyes were stinging, my face clearly riddled with rivulets of makeup. Em was snuggled up in my bed with Jupiter, a book lying across her chest, abandoned to sleep. She roused as I turned on the living room light, knowing that I'd trip over a ball or dog chew otherwise.

"Shit. You look like you had an awful night." Em

rubbed her eyes and Jupiter looked at me with an accusatory glare. I'd interrupted his love fest with Em.

"I'm fine. It's just raining hard and I walked home."

"From the Drive?"

"No, we went to the Cobalt." I went into the bathroom to wash my face and to try to stop my eyes stinging.

"And, yet, you're home alone and not at Hanna's..." Em called out to me and I walked into the bedroom, sitting down next to Jupiter who now thumped his tail against the bed, not yet awake enough to remove his paws from Em's torso but at least demonstrating that somewhere in his core he was pleased to see me.

"No. It was a weird night." I looked up at Em, determined not to cry, having managed to restrain myself on the walk home, even if the rain had given me the perfect cover.

Em could tell that something was wrong, though. That something had happened. She sat up, pushed Jupiter aside and turned to face me, cross-legged. She didn't say anything. She didn't need to. She just took my hand in hers and waited.

"Oh, Em. It's all fucked." I looked down at our hands, stroking the skin between her thumb and forefinger, glad for the sensation of touch uncomplicated by lust.

"Sweetheart, what happened?" Em had this way of quietly prompting speech, even if you had no plans to divulge anything. She knew when you really did need to talk and just weren't allowing yourself to let things out. I both hated and loved her for it. Talking to Em one on one had always been dangerous. At any time you might let something slip that you had not yet admitted to yourself. She was like a human polygraph, except you didn't even know the questions you were unconsciously answering, until you answered them.

"I think I'm in love with Cass."

"Ah."

We were both quiet for a few seconds. Then Em said, "I'll get the gin."

I took off my socks and dumped all my clothes onto the floor, then climbed into pyjamas and into bed. Jupiter promptly fell asleep on my feet.

Em returned and handed me a drink, having procured a lime from somewhere. She must have brought one over. She was so organised.

"So, what happened? Did Hanna get fresh and make you realise you weren't into her after all?" Em smiled, half joking.

"Not quite. We were having a great time, although I was in my head a bit, you know, because it's been a while and it's hard not to think too much." I sipped my gin and laughed. Em patted my knee. "So we were at the Cobalt and we danced a bit and it was all going well. There was even a bit of kissing and ear nibbling." I drank more gin, blushing at the thought.

"So it was going really well! And..."

"And I was just about getting over myself and managed to stop thinking about Janice -"

"Oh. Ah. OK." Em gave me the 'you need to be done with that already' smile. I knew it well, but Janice and I had been together more than half a decade and the rule of thumb is a third of the length of the relationship to be over that person. I almost had a year in the bag. It wasn't enough.

"So. There was ear nibbling and that was all great. Then I went to the bar and she went to the washroom. Well, OK, so first someone knocked into us and so we stopped grinding and kissing and I think I know who knocked into us because I don't think it was an accident."

Em looked puzzled. "Wait. So, what? All was good, and then some ass interrupted and so you broke things off and, what, then you were going to reconvene at the bar right?"

"Right. Except when I was waiting at the bar, Cass arrived." Em actually gasped.

"No! Why? Was she just there anyway?"

"Well, she knew I had a date with Hanna, somehow. But she couldn't have known I'd be at the Cobalt. Anyway, so she pulled me over to the side of the room and, well, and then -"

"What?" I didn't speak. "What did she say?"

"Well, that's just the thing. She didn't say anything, she just pushed me up against the wall and kissed me and wouldn't let me go." I felt the tears starting to fall. "I'm just so fucking angry at her." I was beginning to realise just how pissed off I was at Cass. She had ruined it. She had ruined everything before it had even had a chance to go anywhere. I had still been fine pretending we were friends, pretending it was all cool and that there was nothing between us. She had fucked it all up. "She kissed me, Em. She fucking kissed me but in the worst possible way. She did it out of spite, or jealousy, or anger or some other fucked up thing and not because she actually wanted to or gave a shit about me. If she likes me then she's going about telling me in a really stupid way."

"Did she hurt you?" Em said quietly. She had a calm fury that was terrifying. I loved her even more for that.

"Well, no, I guess not really. But it was scary. You know, not hot or sexy or anything, just really fucking sad and scary."

"Do you... well, are you still into her? Or has this soured everything? Was she really that intense?"

"Yeah. Like, it really was not hot. She really scared me, Em. I don't think I can be around that. I don't want to be around that. She needs to just calm the fuck down and grow up. Maybe I'm not totally over Janice and

60

maybe it was kind of nice to think that Cass and I could be a thing at some point in the future, but that was it, that it was a future thing, when I was ready. Not now. Not like this. She really fucked it all up." I drank the last of my gin and thought about how things were with Janice. There had been that initial burst of passion, of desire, and then we'd quickly fallen into a really comfortable quiet compassion. The intensity had been short-lived and perfect, until it wasn't. "I think I'm just really disappointed."

"You wanted her to be able to wait?"

"Yeah! Exactly. I just thought she got it, you know. I guess I had it at the back of my mind that there was, like, some kind of tacit agreement that we'd just wait and say nothing and just not acknowledge anything but still not fuck each other over, you know."

"Oh, honey." Em smiled a sad little smile and wiped my cheek with the flat of her thumb. "You know how ridiculous that sounds, right?" She waited for me to laugh.

"Yeah." I gulped and laughed and then cried and laughed some more. "I don't know why I thought she just understood somehow, even though we barely know each other. I just thought we got each other. I figured it would be easy, like..."

"Like with Janice?" Em asked, and I nodded.

"But, Kate, things with Janice weren't always simple either. It's easy to remember things otherwise because you miss her but it didn't end well and it wasn't good for you, for either of you."

"But I really fucking love her, Em, you know?"

"Loved her?" Em asked.

"No. That wasn't a slip. I do love her. If she came back right now and asked to come home I'd have her back without any hesitation."

"Sweetheart, you're just saying that because you're

scared and maybe a bit lonely. You have to hold onto the memory of your last few months together. Neither of you were happy. You know that, right?"

"But we were just stuck, we didn't know what else was out there and it seemed better than what we had, but what we had was great. Maybe she sees that now."

"Kate."

"I know. I know. But if she did come back. From wherever the fuck she is right now. Do you know where she is?" Em hadn't been close to Janice but they had been Facebook friends and I'd never really asked her before if she had kept in touch. She looked at me with pity and I scooched down into the bed, not looking at her.

"I don't know. Last I heard, she was in Paris"

"What? Jeez." I'd tried so many times to convince Janice to go on a romantic break with me but we'd always ended up taking vacation time to visit her family in the Kootenays

"That was a few months ago though. I don't have any idea where she is now."

"It doesn't matter. She's not coming back. I should just accept it."

"Well, yeah. I do think it'd be better for you if you did. I mean, you have this hot barista who clearly likes you." Em poked me in the shoulder, trying to make me smile. "You really should just forget about Cass. Maybe you like her, she's pretty attractive and has that whole bad girl vibe, but it seems like she's got lots of shit to deal with and I don't think you need that right now. And, frankly, it's not going to be good for her to be with you if that means she's not going to get called out on her shit."

"You're so wise, Em."

"I try." Em sighed dramatically. "Now, go brush your teeth and let's sleep. That way, we're closer to brunch time and mimosas."

CHAPTER EIGHT

I knew that I'd run into Cass at some point but for the next few days I avoided the parks nearby and, instead, took Jupiter down to the beach, running down Main Street and then taking a long lazy stroll back after some swimming at False Creek. It turns out that avoidance was good for my general health. I was certainly getting more exercise than usual. I was also avoiding the café as Hanna hadn't replied to any of my texts and I figured she was pissed off at me. I guessed that she might have seen me with Cass at the club. I'd be pissed off too if I were her.

On Thursday, three days after my date with Hanna, I sent Em into the café as an emissary. Em talked to Hanna who confirmed that, yes, she had witnessed mine and Cass's Cobalt interaction and had promptly left, figuring that that was about as bad as a date could get. Of course, she had said all this in a slightly less civil fashion. Em spared me the expletive-riddled version but had gotten the point across that Hanna was less than pleased that the person she'd been kissing one minute was kissing someone else the next. I guess I should have explained earlier but it had seemed like an odd betrayal of Cass somehow.

I was thinking about how best to explain things to Hanna as I ran past Dude Chilling Park and back up to Broadway with Jupiter, getting in some exercise before the Friday morning team meeting at work. We stopped as the lights changed near Kingsgate Mall and my ragged breath forced me to bend double and clutch my sides. It was cold today and the freezing air was stinging my lungs more than usual, all those little alveoli contracting and protesting. Jupiter's head was right next to mine and he looked at me pityingly.

"Shut up," I said, and he licked his lips, barely panting. "You've got four legs. You're at least twice as fast as me, so shut up."

I'll admit that I missed the normal park routine where I could stand around and let Jupiter do all the running. I wondered when it would be safe to go back to mine and Cass's traditional haunt. A morning run was definitely healthier than my typical enormous travel mug of coffee I took with me the park. Yes, I'd started drinking coffee again. The uncaffeinated me hadn't seemed like such a good idea after all. The morning exercise and coffee combination was really helping me focus at work and I was thinking, happily, about a new idea I'd had for a client's website when the lights changed and Jupiter started across the road, dragging me with him.

As we reached the south side of Broadway, Jupiter darted across me and I had to swerve to avoid falling over him.

"Dude!" I yelled, and looked over to see what it was that had caught his eye. I dropped the leash. Janice was standing right there on the corner of Broadway and Prince Edward, ruffling Jupiter's ears and smiling at me. I couldn't move. My hand was still outstretched towards

64

her, minus the leash that had pulled me into that position. I swallowed and opened my mouth, then closed it and swallowed again. Janice smiled even more broadly and walked over to me, wrapping her arms around me as I stood stiffly. She was not an apparition. She had substance, but I couldn't feel my hands anymore. I had also lost the power of speech and wasn't sure if I was still breathing or not. Thankfully, the cold air meant I could see my breath. I hadn't died of shock at least. I wasn't a ghost, and nor was my ex.

Janice raised her eyebrows, "Surprise!" She passed Jupiter's leash back to me and carried on scratching his ears as he rubbed up against her legs excitedly. He hadn't seen her in almost a year. I hadn't seen her in almost a year. I felt weirdly numb, unable to really register that she was right there, in front of me, not in Chile, India, Thailand, Paris or wherever.

"You're back," I said, somewhat redundantly.

"Yes. I got in yesterday, figured it was time to get back to work."

"Oh, you kept your job up at UBC?" Why was I talking so normally? How was this so normal suddenly?

"Yeah, they held it open for me, which was nice. And my money started running out so I didn't want to push things too far. Plus, I guess I got what I was looking for and so it didn't seem so important to always be moving about, you know?" I didn't know. I wasn't sure that I wanted to know. Janice going off to find herself had always seemed like a crock of shit to me. I had found her already and I didn't understand why she couldn't see herself as I saw her. I kept telling her she was right there, up until the point where she had screamed at me and walked out. It was the first time I'd really seen her lose it and I guess I had wondered in that moment if you could ever really know anyone fully, if they would always be capable of surprising you.

65

Somehow that seemed dangerous then, now a certain degree of unpredictability seemed necessary in a partner.

"So, um, where are you staying?" I figured she had to be in a hostel or temporary apartment, otherwise whichever friend she was staying with would have warned me she was coming back, wouldn't they? All of our friends were mutual; they hadn't needed to pick sides because Janice had essentially abdicated from numerous friendships when she had flown off and lost contact with people.

"Oh, I met a guy in Mali who has a place here and so I'm crashing there for a bit. Hey, if you know of any cool apartments, or maybe someone looking for a roommate or something, that'd be great." She smiled, her perfect white teeth showing up more than ever against her tan skin. She looked really good. Her hair was longer, wilder. Perhaps Janice had gotten used to life without her ceramic straighteners. Her face was peppered with freckles and she was wearing a long white tunic that did little to disguise her thin frame. I couldn't decide if she was too skinny, unhealthy, or if she was just super lean and toned. I felt a familiar tug of lust but it quickly dampened down again. It was just muscle memory and that muscle had no stamina these days it seemed.

I didn't want to help Janice find an apartment. I didn't want to bump into her in the neighbourhood, or suddenly start seeing her at brunch with friends. I could feel all of the work I'd done this past year just slipping away, the tiny vestiges of confidence and happiness I'd clawed from the wreck of myself just eroding as she smiled her perfect smile at me. She was so fucking unfazed by running into me. She had gone off and had her adventures and left me here like a worthless piece of crap and she knew, she had known that the whole time, that while she was off having fun I would be here doing the same old shit, badly.

66

I needed to not be standing on the corner with my ex. "Sure," I said, "I'll let you know if I hear of anything. Email's still the same, right?" Janice nodded and smiled. "Cool. OK. Well Jupiter and I should be getting home. I have to get ready for a date," I said, and I immediately wondered why I had invented such a thing. There was no date, just work, and Janice would know that. Why did I even feel it necessary to lie about such a thing, and so obviously? It took all the energy I had not to sigh and retract the idiotic statement.

Janice's face contorted into something akin to a smile but more like she was holding in a burp. Her embarrassment for me was obvious. "Nice. Well, enjoy."

"See you around then." I nodded at her and set off running, dragging Jupiter behind me as he and I both pondered Janice's reappearance.

Everything about my exchange with Janice had been painful, awful, shallow, and so very clearly one-sided. She was so over me. She had been for a long time, and I had just acted like a fool, proving I was still incapable of forming real sentences around her, of staying calm.

Once safely back inside my apartment, Jupiter and I sat down with our backs to the front door. I put an arm around his shoulders and told him we were going to have a serious talk. He yawned, licked me face and then stared at me, his nose almost on my eyeball.

"What do you reckon, Jupes, am I still in love with Janice or has that ship sailed? Are we done there?" Jupiter said nothing, making no movement to signify the remotest interest in my life problems.

"I did love her, but who was it that I loved? She didn't really change; at least I didn't think so. Maybe I changed, and then she left. And now she's changed. Have I?" As usual, my wise hound decided not to respond to my nonsensical ramblings.

I stood up and went to my bookshelf. Packed

between two Atwood's was the photo collage Janice had made me for my birthday one year, before things had soured between us. It had pictures of us in the Kootenays, in Europe, visiting my family in the UK, cycling on Salt Spring, and sitting in the hot springs up at Harrison. They were good times. Could we ever really be friends? I had felt a twinge of desire for her just now but had that really meant anything? After all, even before we broke up, the bed death had been glaringly obvious. Everything had felt pretty perfunctory, even for me, and I'd finally just stopped trying to incite any lust from Janice. Maybe I just wanted her back because it was easier than figuring all my shit out. If I had her to tell me who I was then I didn't ever really have to think about it. I had been with Janice for so long that being me had become less of an option. I had turned myself into an appendage through neglect and now I was having phantom body syndrome, only the body had returned and was hotter and, presumably, available.

I shook my head, put the photo back on the shelf, and went to take a shower. It wasn't cold but it did the trick all the same. I emerged from the bathroom entirely set on never seeing Janice again or, at least, not pursuing her, nor being a love-struck dolt around her. We were done. I had to be my own person and to do that I needed to be Janice-free. I should concentrate on work, on being happy in myself. What's more, I realised, that little rustle of lust was nothing compared to the heat that swept through me when I thought about Cass. But Cass had some serious and likely insurmountable issues and so where did that leave me? Hanna.

From this point on, I would go all out. Hanna was hot, smart, funny, kind, and had at least been interested in me. I had allowed Cass to fuck that up and so now I would undo the damage. I was going to bag that barista even if I had to induce a coffee coma in the process.

68

CHAPTER NINE

I was dancing in my kitchen to *Papa Don't Preach* when the buzzer sounded. Jupiter came lumbering out of the bedroom to stand at the door. I wasn't expecting anyone but I buzzed them in anyway, knowing I shouldn't but also knowing that nobody could hear me over the sound of the traffic if I bothered to yell and ask who it was. A video intercom would be great, although pretty unlikely in a cheap East Van apartment. Really, I was just lucky that the buzzer worked.

I stood alongside Jupiter, waiting and peering out of the spyhole. Suddenly Hanna filled my view. I didn't even know that she knew my address. What was she doing here? I'd texted her and gone to the coffee shop but she hadn't been working and had not replied to my messages. I was almost at the point of asking her coworkers if they could get her to call me but now it seemed that I didn't have to.

"Hi." She stood stiffly at the door but then Jupiter started wiggling himself through her legs and she had no choice but to laugh and relax a little.

"Hi. Um, come on in." I held the door open for her and Jupiter led her in, nuzzling her hands. "It's nice to see you. I've been trying to get in touch and explain... things."

She raised an eyebrow, a gesture that was probably not intended to be hot but which was nonetheless. She didn't say anything but I gestured to the couch and offered her a beer, knowing that I needed one.

"Thanks." She took a swig and swallowed hard. Looking up at me, her eyes full of intensity, she said, "So I don't know what happened at the Cobalt but it pissed me off. Maybe I shouldn't have just taken off but, it was just really fucking rude and I have had enough drama so I didn't want to get in the middle of things."

"There's nothing to get in the middle of," I said. "It was a misunderstanding. Well, a mistake I guess. Cass got carried away and took me by surprise and we haven't actually talked since so I still don't really know what her deal is. I thought we were just friends so..."

"Yeah, you didn't look like just friends from what I saw."

I thought back to Cass pushing me up against that wall, her lips on mine, her breath on my neck. I took another gulp of beer. "Like I said, it was a mistake. I didn't know she was going to be there. I didn't know she was going to do that, or even that she was interested, if she actually is."

Hanna snorted. "She looked pretty interested."

"Yeah, I guess. But, I don't know. I did think that she was maybe interested in you and was jealous and so that was why she wanted to fuck things up. I really don't know her all that well." It was true, I had only known Cass about three months and most of our conversations had been about dogs, then dating. Really, we barely knew each other at all.

"I'm pretty sure she's into you. I mean, who

wouldn't be, right?" Hanna smiled, relaxing a little now that she had a better grasp of things. She unzipped her coat and sat back into the couch.

I sat down next to her, cross-legged and sideways, pointing myself at her. "So... does that mean I'm forgiven?"

She clinked her bottle against mine and laughed. "Well, you're too cute right now not to forgive so, yeah."

"Awesome."

"Great."

"Fab."

"Spiffing."

"Really? Spiffing? Really?" I liked that she was mocking me a little and I gently poked her knee with my finger. She clutched at my hand and tessellated our fingers, then pulled me in and kissed me hard. I managed to reach behind me and put down my beer bottle on the back of the sofa and then I slipped my hand round Hanna's waist underneath her coat, the warmth trapped inside.

She also freed up both hands and lifted me over to straddle her, those drummer's arms proving highly adept. I held her head as I kissed her from above and then she evaded my kiss so as to begin moving her lips down my neck to my shoulders, pausing for just a moment to pull my sweater over my head.

"Is this OK?"

"Yes, yes." I kissed her furiously, pushing my body into hers, starting to wonder at how I could possibly remove all of those layers she had arrived in. She helped me out, wriggling free of her own sweater and shirt. There was a tiny tattoo just beneath her right shoulder, so small that I couldn't make out the words. I traced it with my fingers as I kissed her again, and then worked my way round to her earlobes, her neck, the swell of her breasts. I could feel her nipples straining at the thin fabric and I ran my thumbs over the hardness. She undid her bra and then mine too, again asking if it was OK.

"Maybe we should," my words got smushed by her mouth, "ah, relocate?" She lifted me up and then down to the ground where my legs felt insubstantial. As we walked to the bedroom she pressed her body up against mine, her breasts pushed against my back, her hands spanning my belly and then cupping my breasts, brushing the nipples and sending waves of pleasure through me.

We collapsed onto the bed, undignified but happy, and she began tugging at my pants, questioningly. I nodded and helped wriggle free of the rest of my clothes then helped her get naked. Sliding her thigh between my legs and stiffening the muscle she began to grind up against me and I, beneath her, did the same, feeling her dampness and wanting badly to explore her with my tongue and fingers.

She rolled us over so that I was straddling her again and I leaned back as her hands travelled up my body to caress my breasts. I moved to push my mound against hers, rocking back and forth before she slipped a finger between my labia and made me stiffen with delight. As she worked my clit I reached around and slid apart her lips, finding a joyful wetness.

"I want you inside me," Hanna whispered, her eyes closed and her head straining backwards as I ran my fingers down her slit, coating the skin with her juices. I slipped a finger inside her and then another, using my thumb to circle her clit as I pushed in deeper and then slid back out again. Her fingers slipped away from me as she focused on her own pleasure. Hanna grasped at the pillow beneath her, clutching at it harder every time I set her nerves alight, her body pulsating, feverish.

A sheen of sweat formed between Hanna's breasts and I traced my tongue along this line and then began to circle her nipple, before clamping my whole mouth

72

around it, wanting to take all of her into me while I had all of me inside of her. She wanted it too, instructing me to add another finger, then another until I was wrist deep in her and pounding her hard and fast. Astonished as she bucked her hips against me. I moved between her legs, using my free hand to pull back the hood of her clit before dashing the tip of my tongue over the exposed nub. She trembled and her cunt clamped around my hand as I licked and sucked and drew her close to orgasm. Her breath ragged and her hands now holding my hair, she began murmuring "Yes, oh yes. I'm going to come. Yes. Harder. Right there. Yes." Her whole body tensed and shuddered, and she softened around my hand and was silent for a second, gripped by pleasure, her back arching and the crown of her head tipped into the pillow. She didn't tell me to stop though and I drew her back down slowly before sucking hard at her clit and just keeping my hand inside her as she came again, long and slow this time, a little ejaculate pulsing out over my chin as she moaned into the pillow and slammed her hand down onto the bed. This time she said, "Ok. Ok. Stop. Oh. Stop." and I eased my hand free before sliding my body up over hers. I kissed her neck and arms and face and lips while she struggled to open her eyes and rejoin reality.

Looking up at me, her face crowned by a halo of mussed up hair, she simply exhaled. A moment later and she whispered, "Fuck," and then laughed and pulled me closer in so I smothered her face with my body.

After a second or two she rolled me over and asked what I liked, her hands already tracing down over my breasts to my pubis. "I like you," I replied and grasped at her hand, pushing it down to my clit, knowing I was only moments away from my own climax.

As I came, my body contorting and shivering, tiny explosions of light fluttering against my eyelids, I suddenly thought of Janice, of the last time she had made my body feel this way. That was the last time I'd been touched with love and now there was this, with Hanna, who I didn't really know at all but who was sexy and sweet and right here. Hanna, who smelled so good, tasted so good, fit so well next to my body now she was lying beside me. Hanna, with her drummer's arms, her barista's hands. Hanna. Not Janice. Not Cass. I had definitely not just been thinking of someone else's fingers on my body when I came. I wrapped Hanna's hand in mine. It was her I wanted. Hanna. My Hanna. Not Janice. Not Cass.

CHAPTER TEN

I was staring over the top of my coffee cup, watching
Hanna move around behind the counter, when a torso,
clad in plaid, filled my view. I looked up into Em's face,
registering the mildly amused expression.

"What's up?"

"Oh, so you don't know? You've no possibly idea?
No clue at all?" Em sucked in her lips and raised her
eyebrows, eyes wide. She plopped herself down into the
chair opposite me and I waited. She drummed her fingers
on the table, still staring at me.

"Em. I honestly have no idea what you're talking
about."

"Not a tiny sliver of a thought? A kernel of ken? An
inch of insight?"

Em did this sometimes; turning the most basic
conversation into a copywriter's wet dream.

"Not a crumb of clue, no," I said, looking over her
shoulder and smiling at Hanna who had just waved and
pointed at her watch. Her shift ended in ten minutes and
we were going to the Park Theatre to see the new Woody

Allen movie that she had heard good things about. I hated Woody Allen, all that classism and misogyny, but I was pretty sure Hanna would come back to mine afterwards, so Woody could act as foreplay.

"Ahem," Em coughed and then turned to look pointedly over her shoulder at Hanna who was now busy rearranging muffins. "Not a clue, eh?" Em grinned at me and I realised, finally, what she was getting at.

"Oh. Yeah. So Hanna and I hooked up. I guess I should've told you."

Somehow, it had not occurred to me to announce anything to anyone about the other night but Hanna and I had bumped into Kerry at Brassneck brewery yesterday and I guess she'd told Grace, who'd told Em, who was now here looking at me like I was keeping a giant secret.

"So you finally got your barista and, what, you've been ensconced in a little love nest and have only just emerged. That's the only possible reason that I had to hear about this from Grace and that you didn't call me days ago. Wait. When did you hook up? Wasn't she pissed at you about Cass? How did you iron that one out then?"

"She came over to mine unannounced and I just explained that Cass had been a mistake and that nothing was going on and that I was into her and then, well," I laughed, "and then I was into her, you know, like," Em interrupted.

"Yes. OK. I want to know things but not everything. Thanks." She reached over and took a sip of my coffee.

"Hey!"

"What? Friends share things you know."

"Touché."

"So are you, what, like dating now? Making googly eyes over my shoulder I see."

"I guess so. We're actually about to go to the

76

cinema to see some Woody Allen film she's interested in." I gritted my teeth and Em laughed.

"I know you hate him but I have heard good things about this one. I was going to go and see it."

"Well, hey, come along. Hanna won't mind." I wanted to spend some time with Em, we hadn't seen each other in a while and, I thought, maybe she could tell me what was going on with me and Hanna. I didn't fucking know.

"Won't that kill the mood a bit? Or will you guys sit in the back row and suck face while I chaperone in front, eating my popcorn like a spinster?"

"No. It'll be fine. Come with us, unless you're busy or something?"

"I'm free as a bird. Steve's in Toronto for a couple of weeks and so it's just me and Thunderpuss watching *Twin Peaks* on Netflix and drinking half-assed cocktails. A little time out of the house would be good. And you two lovebirds could rekindle the concept of romance in my cranky and ischaemic heart."

"I'm not sure we class as lovebirds. Nor should you take romantic cues from whatever's going on with us."

Em looked at me quizzically. "What, so you're not as into her as you thought?" I shrugged in response. "Shit. It's not, well, it's not that you're still hung up on Janice is it?"

"No. I'm pretty sure that's cool. Although, maybe you already know, she's back. We ran into each other a few days ago."

"No fucking way! Why don't I know anything that happens anymore! Out of the queer loop I guess."

"Em," I said gently, "that's not true. You know I normally tell you everything. I just haven't been talking to anyone really and I haven't really been thinking about Janice. I think I'm still a bit in shock actually." I smiled grimly. "She looks really good you know and she seemed super chatty and relaxed and happy."

"Sickening. I guess that's what a year of living it up on beaches will do for you." Em made a gagging noise and smiled reassuringly. "So is she sticking around or what? Did she say? Did you ask? Where's she living?"

"Er. She's at some guy's place. Someone she met while travelling. She'll be back at her job up at UBC. She's looking for an apartment so if you know of anything..." I paused and then shook my head. "You know what? If you know of a sweet apartment in the 'hood, don't tell me because I'll end up telling her and then we'll be neighbours and I can't deal with that shit."

"Oh. OK. So... not totally over her then?"

"Yeah. I mean no. No, I mean. Ugh. I think I'm in the anger stage of grief. That's normal right? I went through denial and bargaining and now I'm just angry that she left, and that her life's awesome, and that she's just skipping right back into the groove all tanned and lovely and wavy of hair."

"I'm pretty sure anger comes before bargaining but maybe that means you're closer to acceptance. Then again, what the fuck do I know? So she looks good, eh?"

"Yeah. Her hair's long and tousled and... She has tousled bloody hair Em!" I rolled my eyes and then spotted Hanna coming over and tried to adopt a calm demeanour.

"Hey!" She bent down to kiss me and we did an awkward head bump.

"Sorry."

"No worries. Hey, Em, right? Nice to see you again." Hanna smiled at Em who smiled back and then shot me a glance of unknown intent.

"Ready to go?"

"Sure. Oh, hey, so it turns out that Em is also interested in this movie and," I stopped because Em was waving her hands furiously. Hanna turned to look at Em and so she slowed her hands down, fanning herself.

"Hot in here, eh? Yeah, I thought I might see the movie sometime, so you should let me know what you think of it."

"Why don't you come with us? If you're free that is." Hanna shot me a smile and reached out to squeeze my hand on the table. "That's cool, right Kate?"

"Sure, yeah, if it's cool with you?"

"Absolutely. Great. Well, it starts in half an hour so let's go and get in line for tickets." She rummaged in her bag for a second, realised she'd left her umbrella in the back and ran off to retrieve it, leaving me and Em staring at each other in silence.

"You know what?" Em said, "If you don't want her, she's mine."

I scoffed, "Er… Steve?"

"Come on. She's a drummer."

"So you're just going to steal my girlfriend?"

"Oh, so she's your girlfriend now? Two minutes ago you were describing the beauty of Janice's hair and didn't know what the hell you were doing with your lovely barista friend here. A little competition got you all defensive?" Em nudged me as we walked over to the door to wait for Hanna.

"Maybe," I said, coyly. "As if you'd win though Em. I have all that confused and pathetic charm working for me. It really reels in the ladies."

"Clearly." We both laughed and then Em said, "Where's Cass anyway? Didn't you reel her in too?"

All the warmth left my fingers, my hands, my lips. Just thinking of Cass made my body curl in on itself. I hadn't seen her for over a week and it already felt like there was a gaping hole in my head, letting the cold in. I'd been varying my timing at the dog park, deliberately walking past her house in the hopes of running into her but she'd just vanished. We had no mutual friends so I couldn't even find out how she was doing. She was far too cool for Facebook so all internet stalking possibilities were out too. She basically didn't exist online; maybe that's what made her so present, so intense in person.

"I haven't seen her since the Cobalt, er, incident. And she didn't answer any messages so I don't know where she is."

"Oh. Hmm. Well, I'm sure she's fine and she's just letting her ego rest a bit before she resurfaces. A girl like her probably doesn't get too many refusals. And you were pretty clear about not being interested, right?"

"I guess."

"Kate. You're not still thinking you," Em lowered her voice as Hanna was approaching, "you know?"

"No, of course not. It was a mistake."

"What was a mistake?" Hanna slipped her arm into mine.

"Eating that brownie. Your baker needs some schooling."

"Shut up!" She laughed and squeezed my arm as we followed Em out of the door and into the seemingly ceaseless rain.

CHAPTER ELEVEN

Blue Jasmine made me angry, but Hanna enjoyed the movie for all its awkwardness. Em, always the diplomat, appreciated both of our opinions. We went for a drink at Stella's and Em and Hanna shared some fries and talked about *Hannah and Her Sisters*. It turned out that Hanna's dad was a Woody Allen fan too, hence her name. I got lost in the plot twists and blow by blow accounts of what sounded like ludicrous slapstick scenes and so my mind started wandering, first to work, then to Janice, then to the mystery of Cass.

I kept checking back in, sneaking a fry, avoiding the aioli, and wondering at how they could possibly still be talking about the movie. It was cold out on the patio, even under the heaters, and I could happily have gone home and curled up with a book, or some knitting without really giving the classist claptrap another thought, but they just kept going over the scenes again and again until Em finally realised how bored I was and apologised.

She put a hand on Hanna's arm and gestured at me.

"I think maybe we should change the topic of conversation. Little Miss Kate is getting a bit bored it seems. Sorry, love." She smiled at Hanna and then gave me an apologetic face scrunch.

Hanna went to squeeze my leg under the table but it took me by surprise and so my knee jumped and jogged the glasses, spilling beer into my lap.

"Oh shit, sorry." Hanna grabbed napkins and started dabbing at my jeans. I brushed her help away.

"No worries, it was my fault. I'm going to go and hip thrust against the hand-dryer. If our server comes over can you get me another beer?" Em nodded and neither of them spoke as I manoeuvered around the table to head to the washroom. Once I was inside I turned to look back at the table and saw that Hanna's hand was now on Em's arm, the two of them leaning in and laughing. I knew they weren't laughing at me but it stung a little anyway. Was I allowed to be jealous that Hanna liked Em, or that Em liked her? I'd been seeing Hanna less than a week.

I walked, John Wayne-style, across the bar to the washrooms where I splashed water onto my crotch and dabbed at the mess with paper towels. I'd need to wash my jeans when I got home, or at least set them to soak so that they didn't stiffen with beer overnight and smell stale and disgusting in the morning.

As I was thrusting my pelvis at the hand dryer on the wall one of the stall doors opened. I'd thought I was alone in the washrooms and so I started to panic that I might have actually been crooning at the wall fixture as I thrust myself close to it again and again, and again. I tracked the person in the mirror by the dryer and when the angle was right I realised that it was Janice. This had been one of our old hangouts. I guess I should get used to not having them to myself anymore.

I wondered how feasible it was to pretend that I

hadn't recognised her. We were far from that stage of nonchalance though, so I waited for her to look up from washing her hands and then caught her eye in the mirrors. She smiled warmly, shook her hands over the sink and joined me at the dryer.

"Had a little accident?" She laughed and nodded her head towards my crotch.

"Blame Woody Allen," I said, only realising after that this sounded creepy and made no sense.

"Oh. Things really have changed since I left. You always hated him, and now he makes your panties all wet." Janice poked her tongue into the side of her cheek and looked at me suggestively. We shared a nostalgic laugh and she started wiggling her fingers beneath the dryer as I stepped back out of the way.

I leaned against the wall beside her and took in the new look. She had this ruffled-round-the-edges thing going on. No more front-pleated pants or A-line skirts paired with neat little sweaters and button downs. Instead, she was wearing a loose cream knit dress that barely touched her knees and which fell off one shoulder slightly, no bra strap in sight. The colour accentuated her tan, and the freckles that covered her face, which I could see properly now in the bright washroom lights. Her legs were bare but some purple legwarmers poked out from the top of her lace-up calf-high boots that looked familiar.

"Hey! Those are mine!" I pointed at her feet. I thought I'd accidentally thrown out the boots in the post-break-up charity store run but here they were adorning her feet, my ex's feet, and looking really fucking good too.

"Yeah. Sorry. I found them in a pile of stuff that was in storage. You can have them back. I just didn't have anything to go with the dress, you know." She actually bent down to start unlacing the boots, giving me confirmation that she was bra-free as the dress gaped at the front. I put my hands behind my back and pushed myself harder against the wall, quelling an urge to lift her up onto the counter and run my hands up those tan thighs, raising the hem of that dress, seeing what else she wasn't wearing underneath. At this rate, the crotch of my pants was never going to dry.

"It's fine. Keep 'em if you like 'em. I already got a new pair. You can't not have boots in Vancouver, right?"

She retied the boots and then stood up, falling towards me in a moment of orthostatic dizziness. As my hands were trapped behind me I found myself pinned, her hands having shot out on either side of me to steady herself.

"Oh, ah," Janice softly exclaimed, her lips close enough that I could feel her breath on my face. I had woken up next to her for years and the proximity of her again was mesmerising. It was as if my brain was erasing the last twelve months, just bringing me back to a place of comfort, joy, love. I wondered what she was thinking, if she felt the same, and then I didn't have to wonder any more as she kissed me, lightly at first and then hungrily when I responded. I drew my hands out from behind me and thrust them into that mass of wonderful hair, enjoying the feeling of Janice, but not Janice, up against me. Her body was muscular now, not just thin but with a soft, world-weathered strength. She wanted me in a whole new way and that was intoxicating.

We pulled our lips apart briefly, my hands still tangled in her hair, hers on my shoulders holding me against the wall. Breathing hard and fast we said nothing, diving back into each other. I knew anyone could come in at any time but I dropped my hand to the small of her back and walked her over to the counter, hoisting her up to sit with her legs apart, my face now buried in her neck, her hair draped across me as I kissed that bare shoulder.

84

Kissing her, touching her, felt like visiting a simulation of home, everything looking and smelling and feeling almost exactly the same but with a sheen of difference that was barely real, that eluded explanation.

"K," Janice's voice tumbled down to me from above, her mouth pointed at the ceiling as I worked my way around her throat with my kisses. "K? Kate?" She was pushing me away, readjusting her dress to cover her shoulders and thighs as she brought her legs back together and dropped down from the counter. She suddenly adopted her 'we should talk' face and it all started coming back to me; the nitpicking, the nagging, the way we could barely even decide what to make for dinner or what movie to watch on date night. All those little things that are code for so much more, so much unsatisfied desire, longing. So much need to step outside of the self built within the confines of coupledom.

I said nothing, just closed my eyes and sighed heavily. She took my hands in hers and I opened my eyes again, a grim smile on my face. We couldn't do this. I would make her unhappy again and then I would be unhappy when she left which she would, inevitably.

"Kate, I want you... but," she said.

"I know. It's OK. I want you too but it's different, right? It feels different." I couldn't reconcile the new Janice with the old and my desire for her now with the nostalgia to be back where we were when things were good. I wondered what she was thinking, why she had stopped kissing me, had pulled back just now.

"Do you think -?" Janice let the question hang in the air.

"We could be friends?" I laughed, and she smiled and squeezed my hands. "Yeah, I think we could you know. Just don't steal any more of my boots, OK." I freed my hands from hers and then wagged a finger at her reproachfully. She hugged me and said we should meet up soon, in a nicer environment than the washroom. I went back to the dryer and lingered for a while, preserving the memory of Janice's lips on mine, the feeling of her hair against my cheek, the new scent of her still holding traces of the old Janice, my Janice. Could we really be friends or was there still some passion there, some desire that would make things too messy? I really had never been the kind of woman to hook up with people in washrooms, or to cheat on a girlfriend and this thing with Janice, however much it was confusing me, had made a couple of things clearer: I didn't want to mess Hanna around and I was not ready to let Janice go, not entirely.

CHAPTER TWELVE

Grace grimaced in concentration as she added Kahlua and vodka to the cocktail shaker. Kerry was trying valiantly to carry on a conversation with me, while simultaneously keeping a studious eye on her girlfriend's progress. Cocktails were Kerry's domain but Grace had decided she needed to learn. I had an inkling that this was some kind of homework exercise from therapy; Kerry surrendering control and Grace trying to be more resourceful, independent, and forthright. I wondered if there was a specific kind of therapeutic approach for tops and bottoms. Did switches just totally confuse queer-centric therapists?

"Sorry, what?" Kerry and I had both phased out and now neither of us could remember what we'd been talking about. I decided to switch the conversation to what we were both actually focusing on anyway: Grace.

"How's my espresso martini coming? I hope you're making it nice and strong. I need it after the week I've had."

"Hadn't you given up caffeine and booze?" Kerry

asked, her eyes still on the cocktail shaker, ready to catch it should Grace's shaking technique go awry.

"Yeah. That was Monday morning. Then reality set in. And, when you're dating a barista who is in a band I don't think it's humanly possible to not drink or caffeinate." I took the finished martini from Grace and sipped. "This is really good! You can make these for me anytime you like. After all, it's more efficient than two beverages and I'm all about efficiency these days." I thought about how quickly Janice and I had reached an agreement in the washrooms at Stella's, and then I laughed at the memory, causing Kerry and Grace to stare at me inquisitively. I hadn't told them yet about my encounter with Janice. I also hadn't told Em. After our second beer, Em had left, saying she had a headache. Hanna had left shortly after, pleading an early shift.

I had briefly wondered if Em and Hanna had actually reconvened afterwards and was a bit surprised at Hanna not coming home with me. Then I felt a twinge of guilt for doubting her when it was me who had just been fooling around with Janice. Anyway, it wasn't like we were being exclusive, at least I didn't think so. My biggest concern was actually Em. As far as I knew, she and Steve had not talked about having an open thing and with Steve away and things not seeming so great between them I wasn't sure how Em was doing.

"What are you laughing at?" Grace asked. "Not my cocktail-making skills, I hope." She laughed but there was a frisson of desperation in her tone.

"No, sweetheart, the martini is seriously good. I really could just do with having a clone of you to set up a bar in my house. No, scrap that, a pocket you to make martinis whenever one is necessary."

"So, all the time then?" Kerry said, pointedly.

"Wouldn't they end up being really small martinis if I was pocket-sized?" One of the things I loved about

Grace was her ability to run with even the stupidest of my ideas.

"I guess pocket-you would have to make lots of martinis on a continual basis." I paused and murmured, "Hmm, do pocket-sized clones have labour rights?"

"They might unionise! How terrifying would that be?" Grace looked genuinely afraid of the entirely fictitious situation we had just created involving picketing pocket-bartenders. Kerry was characteristically silent. She swirled her cocktail in her glass, only having had one sip while I was already halfway down mine. I slowed down, not wanting to confirm my reputation as a lush, nor make it too obvious that Kerry was not really drinking her cocktail.

"So I think Em might be interested in Hanna. And, I think Hanna might be interested in Em." This would distract them for a while.

"What?! But. Aren't. Well." Grace spluttered. She was, and always had been, extremely monogamous and didn't really understand those who weren't. Kerry's previous relationships had had an air of openness about them, although I got the impression that this wasn't official or healthy and had probably been borne more of trust issues rather than joyous compersion. Kerry looked at me with interest but said nothing. She gulped down some of her cocktail.

"Yeah. Well, Hanna and I aren't exclusive and we went to the movies with Em the other night, and then for drinks and they just got on so well and, well, you know. I think they'd be great together."

"But what about Steve?" Grace finally got the words out, sneaking a sly glance at Kerry and then draining her own cocktail. Kerry headed to their bar and began filling their second cocktail shaker to make something decadent and accomplished.

"I don't know. Nothing's going on with Em and

Hanna. I shouldn't have even said anything and I might be completely wrong. I'm just saying that maybe it should or could. Steve's away so it's not like he and Em will be talking about things like that right now."

"And that doesn't bother you?" Grace asked, absent-mindedly taking the cocktail proffered by Kerry and handing her the empty martini glass.

"Nope. Why would it?"

"Are you just saying that because you're not actually that into Hanna?"

I looked at Kerry as she handed me the glass and met my eyes, waiting for me to answer her question. She might have a point, and I was pretty sure she knew it. After all this time thinking about Hanna, mooning over Hanna, and then finally hooking up, it seemed that I might now not be all that interested in her. This clearly was not the point of an open relationship, and I, like Grace, definitely erred towards monogamy, wanting to pour myself entirely into the other person and have them do the same in return.

It was Grace who broke the silence by asking, "Kate, what's going on, really?"

"I think I'm not actually that into Hanna," I said quickly, before guzzling my new cocktail.

"But!" Grace was in a perpetual state of shock tonight it seemed.

"I know. I know. I'm fickle."

"Is there someone else then? You're not still hung up on Janice are you? Oh sweetie, you really need to let that go, she's not coming back."

I laughed at Grace and said, "Well, actually she's back already. But we've already cleared the air and that's all done with." Grace's mouth was actually gaping at this point and Kerry laughed and then gently closed her girlfriend's mouth with a delicate cupping of her chin.

"I think you're giving Grace a heart attack with all

your news. You forget, Kate, we're old and can't take these kinds of shocks anymore."

"Sorry. It's been an eventful week," I said. It was typical how life seemed really slow and trudging for a while and then suddenly you were getting over one woman, sleeping with another and pining after someone else. Well, maybe that wasn't so typical.

I filled Grace and Kerry in on Janice's return, without mentioning what had happened in the washroom at Stella's. Then I tried to explain what was going on with Hanna and me, but as I talked I realised that I didn't really know what I was saying. None of it seemed to make any sense without talking about Cass. Why was she even a factor in this? Cass was a friend. Had been a friend. Now I didn't know.

I figured it was only because I was confused about Janice and that it had been almost three weeks since I'd last seen Cass and I missed her, even if she had behaved awfully that night at the Cobalt. The mornings were not quite the same without our almost daily run-ins in the dog park. There was an odd mix of distance and immediacy between us, a product of the nature of our meeting, in isolation. I had always been alarmingly honest with Cass and it was liberating. It was like we had skipped the teething period of friendship and gone straight to intimacy, without actually really knowing anything about each other.

We had practically ignored each other for the first few weeks after I'd moved into the neighbourhood but when you're on the same schedule as another dog person it's pretty much impossible to avoid interaction, unless you switch to another park. Cass had always had a far-away look, indifferent to her surrounding, sometimes writing in her little black notebook while her dog sniffed his way around the park. She almost always had headphones in and always had a coffee mug with her, which she'd carefully place on the ground as she picked up her pooch's poop.

Over those first few weeks, we had gradually closed the distance across the park, our dogs not yet interacting, just looking at each other warily. Cass was way too cool to talk to me and I was way too shy to make a move. I also knew how precious dog park time can be, how sometimes you just want to be alone with your dog, having a simple interaction with them, not with the world at large. It's a big deal to let someone cut into that time.

Eventually, Cass's dog stole Jupiter's tennis ball and Jupiter sat expectantly in front of Cass, waiting for her to throw the Frisbee in her hand. We exchanged glances as I approached her to apologise and she took out her earphones and said, easy as anything, "Hey." Looking back now it was incredible to think how this little upward glance, an acknowledgement of my being, had such a profound effect on my engagement with my new neighbourhood as well as my newly single status. It was Cass's 'hey,' most likely inconsequential to her, which had made me even vaguely consider life after Janice. Cass had announced herself in a way that was so low-key that it snuck in under my radar, an incipient connection with possibility.

As those first fall colours crept across the park, Cass and I had begun to talk about more than just the dogs: discovering why our schedules were similar; why Cass was such a mess some mornings; the bad dates we'd been on; the good dates we'd been on and why that messed us up more than the bad ones because neither of us could really imagine the possibility of things working out with someone. Cass had been the first one, the only one of my friends to notice when I finally removed my engagement ring, months after Janice had left.

For me, everything came back to Janice, or the ghost of Janice past; that one relationship having set my expectations for every woman I had dated since.

Cass had the opposite problem, never having managed to really commit to any one woman. I suspected that this was because the women she went for were often younger, inexperienced, expecting too much of her and allowing her to feel like a failure as a mentor rather than a success as an equal. She mentioned exes and I lost track of them, their names, the bands they were in, the crazy shit they'd pulled. She talked of things that I had only read about in novels, or not at all. She was Cass and she had reeled me in, been weird about Hanna, pulled that shit at the Cobalt and then disappeared.

I didn't want to say any of this to Grace and Kerry, of course. They would only blow it out of proportion and think I was in love with Cass or something. And I didn't want to tell them about what really happened with Janice because I still wasn't sure how I felt about her. Instead, I tried to switch the focus back to them and the kitten that would be arriving in a matter of days. The great thing about cute animals is that you can usually rely on them to hijack any conversation. This time, though, it didn't work.

"Oh, hey, so we saw that friend of yours. The one that was at the Biltmore that time and was trying to steal Hanna from you. I guess that didn't work out too well for her, hey! Hah!" Grace laughed and then looked at Kerry, "What was her name? You were talking to her... what was it?" Grace was joshing my arm but stopped when Kerry pulled her away.

"What's up, Kate? What's the deal with Cass?"

"Where did you see her?" I asked Kerry, trying to sound nonchalant but knowing that my body language was betraying me. I had drawn my knees up to my chest at the mention of Cass's name and now I slowly lowered them and uncrossed my arms, taking a quick gulp of the cocktail. "When was this?"

"Oh, a couple of days ago. I didn't really speak to her, Kerry did. It was just at Wallflower. We were waiting in line for brunch and she walked past and saw us and sort of did a double take. It was weird actually, like she was going to walk past but then came and talked to us. She asked about you. That was a bit odd as we figured you'd been seeing her. Don't you see her at the park and hang out and stuff?"

"Grace..." Kerry was giving her girlfriend a warning look. A knowing look.

"What?" Grace glanced at both of us, confused. "What did I say? What's going on? Am I missing something?"

I had to put her out of her misery, at least partly. "It's fine. I just haven't seen her for a little while. I guess we keep missing each other and maybe needed some space or something. We'd been spending quite a bit of time together so maybe things got a bit confused."

"Confused, like, with feelings for each other?" Kerry was always so fucking on point it was annoying.

"How about another cocktail!" I said, trying to distract them but, again, they were having none of it. "OK. So what did she say?" I was curious even if I didn't want to admit it.

"Just that she'd been lying low and hadn't seen you and wondered how you were doing," Grace said.

"And you told her I was OK, right?"

"Er, yeah. Of course. Should we not have said that?" Grace wafted her arms around, not sure of what I was getting at.

"No, no, that's fine. I just..." I didn't want Cass to think that everything was fine but at the same time I didn't want her to think that I was pining after her, even if I was. It was nice to know that she was at least a little interested in my well-being though, enough even to talk to people she didn't even know. "So she didn't say where she'd been?" I asked.

"No. What? Why? So when did you last see her?" Grace was now very interested in this whole drama and while I wanted to stop talking about it I also wanted to squeeze out everything I could from them about Cass.

"Oh, about three weeks ago. At the Cobalt. I was there with Hanna, on our first date actually. I ran into Cass."

"And, what, you haven't seen her since?"

"Nope." I buried my face in my drink and then went to their bar, staring blankly at the options until Kerry rescued me. She mixed another round of espresso martinis, the shaking of the ice providing a welcome break from talking.

"So did you have a fight or something?" Grace said. Then, her mind clearly doing some gymnastics, she said, "Oh, shit! So Cass saw you with Hanna and, what, was jealous, right? Because she was after Hanna! Ah, I see now. No wonder she was weird and has been avoiding you."

Grace clearly felt she'd cleared up the mystery and I wasn't about to convince her otherwise but Kerry gave me a knowing glance and I wondered if they'd be talking about me after I left. They had better things to think about though, surely. I might be endlessly fascinating to myself but I figured that my friends could get by without analysing my melodrama every night.

Now that Grace was satisfied with her understanding we moved on to discussing kittens. The shelter was dropping off a two month-old furball the next day and Kerry and Grace showed me the toys, and basket, and treehouse, and litter box, and other accoutrements they had acquired for their new family member. I found myself wondering why they had never had kids. Perhaps they still would. They weren't premenopausal yet, and their nesting instinct was in full bloom. I realised that this was probably the last time that an evening at theirs would have me as the focus. Next time, there would be a kitten climbing my leg or knocking something over or throwing up in a corner and, now I thought about it a little more, I was fine with that. Sometimes, frankly, I bored myself. If I could just get all my shit figured out and be happy then things would be much better. I suddenly felt both tedious as a friend and rather insignificant as a human being. Where was that kitten to distract me with some cute antics?

CHAPTER THIRTEEN

Cass could be infuriatingly obtuse sometimes, especially by text message.

"Park in ten?"

That was all Cass's message said.. I was tempted to throw my phone across the bedroom, but Jupiter was not yet awake and I didn't want to start the day off with a bang. Well, not that kind of bang anyway.

Did she really expect me to just roll out of bed and meet her with so little notice? Annoyingly, I realised that she actually could expect me to do that as I'd done it many a time before. I also texted her first thing to try to time our park trips perfectly. It was always irksome when I arrived just as she was leaving, or vice versa. This time, though, I really did not want to feel that pull towards her, but it was there anyway.

I crawled from under the covers and avoided standing on Jupiter's head as he looked up at me from his pile of blankets. He could have slept longer as we'd had a fairly late night walk, dodging skunks and errant drunken cyclists at midnight when I hadn't been able to sleep because of a certain silent Cassandra who I couldn't stop thinking about.

"Come on Jupes, time to get up and at 'em. Early bird, worm-catching, etc." He thumped his tail against the side of my bed but still didn't bother standing until I was trying to get my socks on, at which point he jumped up to help by sniffing my feet and tickling them, almost making me fall back into bed. Clever boy.

Was I just walking into drama if I went to the park and saw Cass? I wondered what she could possibly say to me. She'd waited almost a week before getting in touch. Maybe she thought I'd be less angry at her by now and would come running into her arms. Maybe she assumed that things hadn't worked out with me and Hanna and that I was fair game again. Not that that had stopped her while I was actually on a date with Hanna. Maybe I should just get back under that warm duvet.

I let her know I was coming, texting simply, "Sure." I didn't want to have her think I had forgiven her. I hadn't. Not really. Not yet. Even if I did forgive her, it could never work out while she acted like such a douche. Cass was a cad and that was fine for those who wanted someone caddish, but I wanted her to be serious. Serious about me. It would never work. I had tried to convince myself that it was worth it just for the fun but I knew better. I had a hard time being lighthearted about things, especially about people, particularly about Cass.

It was freezing out this morning. I tried to keep my hands in my pockets as much as possible, but Jupiter was particularly gung-ho now that he was awake, pulling me along, threatening to tear the seams of my coat pockets if I didn't hold the leash out in the cold. I kept telling him to heel, but to no avail. It was actually quite reassuring to have his exuberant bounce a little ahead of me this morning. It meant that it was basically impossible to start

98

the day grumpy when there's this handsome animal who is super excited to run barefoot in the frost to chase a grotty stick.

We crunched our way across to the park, the silver-white surface of the spongy leaf piles accommodating our footprints: woman and dog, side by side. Jupiter could clearly smell Hobbes, and probably Cass too, as he lunged around the corner to the park, dragging me along. I hadn't the will to fight as I was storing up emotional reserves for when I actually saw Cass.

She was already in the park beneath the tree with the broken rope swing. There was a cloud of white obscuring her face but this wasn't her warm breath in the cold air, I thought. This was probably her morning jay. The pale dawn light crept over the tops of the houses to the east and now it hit the frost at Cass's feet, casting a shadow across the white ground. Cass and the tree stood in silhouette, statuesque for a second or two until she turned and saw us approach. I watched her take a gulp of her coffee and another drag on the joint. She was hunkered down into her sweater, the thick knit Fair Isle, off-white and black. I had come to love that sweater and the cosiness it embodied; how it wrapped around her and sealed in all that was Cass. I wanted to curl myself up under that sweater, nudge my way into the crook of her arm. Or, I guess, I had wanted that, because now I didn't. Now I wanted her to apologise for being an ass, and for being aggressive, and for us to just go back to being dog park buddies and nothing more. I did not want her kind of drama in my life. I hadn't even wanted it in my early twenties and I was sure as shit too old for it these days.

Cass nodded at me, briefly making eye contact, her whole body taut, her shoulders almost up to her ears as she held her coffee cup against her body with one hand and balanced her smoke, which I realised now was just a cigarette, in the other hand. Jupiter had found a stick under the tree and was busily shredding it while Hobbes stared at him, still poised in a play bow that remained unanswered. Even the dogs were failing to communicate.

"Hey," I said, "how's it going?"

"Yeah. Good. You?"

"Fine."

We shuffled our feet a little and I waited for her to say something, anything, but the silence spread like fine frost between us. Jupiter brought me the stick to throw and I hurled it as far as I could, wrenching my shoulder a little in the process. I'd pay for that later.

"You alright?" Cass glanced at me as I rubbed my shoulder.

"Not really. No. I'm a bit pissed off at you actually." Cass laughed and I stared at her in disbelief. "That's funny? You think it's funny that you made me angry?"

"No. No. Just that I meant your shoulder. Is your shoulder alright. You're, like, rubbing it and stuff." She smiled at me as if she cared and I had an urge to just walk away. She was so fucking resistant to taking anything seriously. She invited me here and I had the stupidity to think it was so she could apologise but she was actually just trying to make everything seem normal. It wasn't normal. She'd basically assaulted me and she thought that was fine, that it wouldn't really change anything.

"Fuck off, Cass. Where's my apology?" I stared at her, not quite believing that I'd just said what I'd said. I wasn't normally able to be this forthright, especially not with the women I liked, but then I had never really liked someone like Cass before.

She narrowed her eyes and peered at me. "Dude? What's up? Sorry if I upset you somehow."

"You're serious? You don't know why I'm annoyed at you?"

She shrugged and kicked the ball for Jupiter.

"You practically assaulted me at the Cobalt because you're pissed off about me and Hanna hooking up, right?" I stared at her, my arms folded, my breath quick.

Cass laughed again, although she looked far from happy. "Kate, calm down, I was just high and shit and you just happened to be there is all. Go bang your barista if you love her so much. What do I care?" She broke off eye contact and blew out some smoke away from me.

This time I did turn away. I called Jupiter and we headed out of the park away from Cass, away from the gaping fucking hole of sadness that was opening up under that tree. I actually thought she cared and now she was playing everything so calm and nonchalant. Well, fuck her and her bullshit breeziness. Fuck her.

She called my name, but I didn't look back, and she didn't call again. She had sounded more amused than pleading anyway, I thought. Fuck you, Cass. We're so done.

CHAPTER FOURTEEN

The next day, when I got back from work, Em was once again standing at my front door. She had keys but she had obviously been waiting for me. "I should get you a little bench out here with your name on it," I said, but she just smiled grimly, looked a bit panicky and didn't greet me with her usual hug.

"Hey. Can we go in? Do you have anything to drink? I thought about bringing some whisky and then didn't but maybe I could go and get some. I could. Maybe I could. Should I?" She looked at me wide-eyed.

"Let's go in. I have booze. It's OK." I took her hand and squeezed it while opening the door.

"Sorry. I need to talk to you and I'm a bit anxious."

"Em. Honestly, it's fine. If you're going to say what I think you're going to say then you don't have to worry. Seriously. I'm cool." I smiled at her in what I hoped was a reassuring fashion.

"Really?" She was holding my hand as we stood inside the doorway of my apartment. I let go of her so as to pour us both drinks.

Without looking at her I asked, "Is it about Hanna?"

She said nothing but when I turned to hand her a whisky with ice she was staring at her feet and poking the toe of her left shoe into the floor, twisting it over and over.

"Em? I haven't talked to Hanna today but she didn't come home with me the other night after the movie and I'm pretty sure she's into you even though she hasn't said as much." I paused and then asked gently, "So, you like her, right?"

Again, Em stayed silent and I took this as an affirmative. "Em, it's fine. Hanna and I are barely dating and I don't think it's a long-term thing anyway. The only thing I'm worried about is you. Is this what you want? Really? Are you thinking of leaving Steve?"

Em gasped and shook her head, clutching at her drink, "No! No! I love him, I do. We talked a while ago about me maybe dating women and him, well, he's actually... maybe I shouldn't say."

"Maybe you don't need to." Em's hesitation at telling me something made it pretty clear that it was something Steve might be a bit uncomfortable about people knowing right now. I'd always gotten a bit of a queer vibe from him and I guessed that this was what Em was trying not to divulge. I wouldn't push it. If they wanted to be open about things then they would be, and I'd be there for them when they were ready. "So have you talked to Steve about Hanna? Do you guys have any rules set up?"

"Er, no. We didn't get that far. And with him being in Toronto right now it's, well, it's not really the kind of conversation that you have over Facetime, you know?"

I laughed, imagining the fun of time delays and the connection cutting out at a crucial point in a relationship talk. "I guess not. But you'll talk to him when he's back this weekend, right?"

"Yeah. But I don't really know what to say. Are you sure you're cool with this? I mean, you were lusting after Hanna for so long and now I'm butting in and I've already got Steve. Am I just being greedy? Gah! This is ridiculous."

"It's not ridiculous at all Em. And it's not greedy. You and Steve build your relationship however you like. It's no one else's business as long as whoever you guys hook up with are on board and everyone's safe and… shit, when did I start sounding like an adult?"

We stood in silence for a couple of seconds and then burst out laughing. Then I said, jokingly, "Well fuck you, Em, for taking all the good people while I have no one!"

"I'm sorry sweetheart. You'll find someone. I know it. And, hey, I mean, would it be weird for both of us to be seeing Hanna?" Em asked.

"That might be a bit strange, yes. Anyway, I was thinking of breaking things off with her next time I see her. I don't think I'm being very fair. I think she's awesome and I hope that she's cool with our thing just having been some fun on the way to something else but I think I got a bit over invested in her without really knowing what her deal was or what was really going on with me." I wrinkled my nose. "I guess I've been doing that a lot lately."

"So, it's really OK?"

"Yup! Well, I mean it is if you and Steve work things out, obviously. I'm totally fine with you pursuing something with Hanna, as long as it's not going to mess up stuff with Steve." I gave Em a hug and then asked if she wanted to stay for dinner, hoping she'd say yes so that I had a reason to make something good instead of just eating chips and houmous and then feeling like crap later. One of the toughest things about living alone was learning that it's entirely proper to cook yourself good food. I'd gotten better at it, but my recent endeavours to focus on work and impressing my bosses had left my cupboards a bit bare and my takeout delivery guys a bit too familiar. Em was only too happy to stay, now that her revelation had gone so well. She was already fixing us another drink. What a trooper.

CHAPTER FIFTEEN

It was time, I decided, to take a break from dating. Now I wasn't seeing Hanna I was actually enjoying having time on my own and not worrying about lining up dates and making a good first impression and where my night would end up. Jupiter was happy that I was home more often and less stressed. I had actually started saving money too, and had even bought myself membership at the Float House. Dating was an expensive business. An investment in my future, perhaps, but right now the market conditions seemed pretty poor so I'd stuff that money under my mattress and hold tight. I was much more engaged at work too. In fact, I had finally learnt the names of most of the other contractors and the permanent staff, and had realised I had been horribly self-involved and gloomy in my time there. It clearly paid to be invested; my boss had even asked me to work on a new project for a much-prized client. I hadn't even realised the guy knew my name, much less the work I'd been doing for them this past year.

I was feeling strangely grown up this week. Work

was going well. I had shopped for groceries. My talk with Hanna had even been mature and considered and had worked out splendidly. We met in the park the day after my conversation with Em and as I tried to avoid saying "It's not you, it's me," Hanna had gingerly admitted to being interested in Em. We stood in the Vancouver drizzle, warming ourselves with coffee, and she apologised for things not working out. Then Jupiter bounded towards us, scattering mud everywhere. Hanna and I laughed, hugged and clearly both felt relieved that we were breaking up drama-free and could stay friends. I really wished I could have told Hanna that Em was interested in her too. I'd have to give Em and Steve a kick in the pants if they didn't make some decisions soon. It seemed all too easy for poly primaries to be horribly self-involved and forget about their seconds, and thirds, and all those other awful words to describe the other people in their lives. I was pretty sure Em and Steve would do just fine though, they were both such kind people, barely ever putting themselves first.

In addition to, apparently, getting my entire life back on track and becoming a voice of reason to friends, I'd started hanging out at the coffee shop again, not caring if I ran into Cass. I felt oddly immune to her charms, having realised that, as much as she might want to, she didn't seem capable of caring for anyone other than herself right now.

I had seen Cass and Hobbes in the park a few times, but I definitely had the impression that she was trying to avoid me still. She always looked so sad and closed off, and, while I wondered what was going on with her, I had decided to just leave her to figure her shit out. I hadn't had a chance to tell her I'd broken things off with Hanna, or that banging the barista had not been quite the mistake she had made it out to be. I figured Cass would be happy to be proven wrong this time, and to know that

107

it was safe to keep frequenting the coffee shop. At least, that is, I was frequenting it. Hanna told me that Cass had only been in once or twice in the past week and had left before she had had a chance to talk to her. Maybe Cass was deliberately avoiding us both, or the world at large.

After a while, I really did begin to worry about Cass though, and Jupiter and I spent longer and longer in the park each day, hoping to run into her and Hobbes. I wanted to give her a chance to talk, not really knowing if she had anyone else to talk to. Anyone but a past lover, that is. Then they disappeared completely and, when I hadn't seen them for over a week, I was tempted to text. It seemed a little desperate, and although I really wanted Cass to know that Hanna and I had broken up I was certain that Cass and I shouldn't be dating, so maybe this space was good for us both.

Eventually, my concern outgrew my pride and I gave up trying to play it cool and sent Cass a text to say that I missed her and Hobbes and hoped everything was OK. She didn't reply and so I waited a couple of days and then texted again, asking if she was alright. This time I just got a response saying "Yeah, just busy. See you around." It looked pretty obvious that Cass was not interested in talking to me right now.

It was Kerry who told me that she'd heard from a friend that Cass wasn't doing so great. She'd pretty much stopped partying, trying to kick the molly and even quitting smoking. I guessed that her depression had taken hold and, coupled with withdrawal, I could see why she was avoiding company. Em suggested that I stop pussyfooting around and just go to Cass's house. I was still her friend, after all. So, I figured I'd drop by, see how she was doing and, if the opportunity arose, I could nonchalantly let it slip that Hanna and I weren't seeing each other anymore and maybe we could hang out like old times at Our Town for coffee between classes.

108

Maybe then Cass would see a little more daylight and stop worrying about running into the two of us and having to make nice.

I walked over to Cass's place under the pretext of returning a book which I knew wasn't actually something she had lent me. My bag was heavy with a growler newly acquired from Brassneck, the latest craft brew-pub to crop up in town. I hoped Cass would invite me in for a drink and wouldn't simply turn me away at her door.

Cass's place was one of those Vancouver-style so-called-garden suites that actually sat below ground. This souped-up basement, complete with damp and vermin was reached by a set of unlit steps which I now walked down rather gingerly, trying to stop Jupiter from pulling me over.

I knocked on the apartment door and the frosted glass rattled in the rotting doorframe. I thought of how much cold air must be creeping into Cass's place right now, how cold she must be. I shuddered both at the thought and through nervousness. My knocking had alerted Hobbes, who I could hear shuffling about behind the door. Cass yanked the door open and frowned at me. It wasn't quite the welcome I'd hoped for. Of course, Hobbes gave Jupiter a much happier welcome as they bumped noses and wiggled around me and Cass, almost knocking me over.

"Hey!" I said and smiled, holding out the book. "I brought this. I think you gave it me a while back. Sorry for not returning it sooner."

Cass took the book and said thanks, without even looking at it. Hmm. I guess that plan backfired. At least I had already read it.

I tried my second mode of attack, brandishing the growler, full of a cherry sour. "Busy? Care for a little tipple?" I could see that she was trying not to let me in but I was determined. "If you're studying then it's obviously time to take a beer break. And, if you're not studying then it's obviously time to drink more beer. Yes? You can't argue with me." I carried on grinning, my face beginning to hurt in the freezing air. "C'mon Cass, let me in already, Jupiter would be freezing his nuts off if he still had any." Finally she cracked, laughing at the sad neutered dog, and she stood aside to let me in. Jupiter barrelled past her to sniff the unfamiliar house that smelled like a familiar friend and I followed, taking note of the cold damp air, feeling grateful I wasn't a student working for a non-profit.

As Hobbes gave Jupes the grand tour I took in the tiny studio apartment, complete with one overflowing bookshelf, a sofa bed with a tangle of bed sheets littered with papers, and a ragged couch that looked like it had once lived with a cat. The real winner in terms of décor, however, was the coffee table, strewn with beer cans and smoking paraphernalia. I guessed that the detox wasn't going well.

"Been on a bender?" I nodded at the table and laughed.

"No more than you'd expect," Cass replied, as she reached for a couple of clean glasses from the cabinet above her sink. For a second I wondered what she thought I thought of her, then I just wondered how she could bear to live in this dingy little place. I needed light. I would go crazy without light. I guess, with school and work, she was hardly ever here during the day, and it was quiet at least, hidden away from the world. Plus, if she was partying again, she would be sleeping most of the day away on weekends, so it probably didn't matter too much if it was dark. Maybe it was actually better for her.

"So, what have you been up to? Any hot new ladies hiding under that bed of yours?" I pretended to peer beneath the sofa bed, noticing that there were more books piled under there too. Some actually seemed to be

110

holding up part of the bed.

"Yeah. Something like that." Cass handed me the glass, having carefully poured the beer to minimise the head. Her non-committal responses were making me nervous and I wondered how long I could maintain this cheer in the face of such stony opposition.

"Do you have papers due? Am I actually interrupting studying? Sorry. I just wanted to see you. I haven't seen you for a while and I was, if I'm honest, starting to wonder if you were OK, if you were avoiding me maybe?" I laughed, trying to make it sound like a joke but looking at her to see if any twitch of her face would reveal that this really was the case.

"Just busy. School and work and shit. You know." Cass flicked her eyebrows and twitched her mouth into a slight side-smile. She sipped her beer and went to sit on the sofa, sinking into it and pushing her feet carefully into the mess of the coffee table, clearing a little space with her toes. She had holes in the bottom of her socks and I realised that I'd never really seen her feet before. We had never been in a private space, never shoeless, never sockless. These tatty socks made her seem vulnerable, not the self-assured, cocky Cass I was used to.

I realised that I'd never actually seen any of Cass's skin aside from her hands and face. She was like an unknown mime artist to me, albeit dressed in button downs and Fair Isle sweaters and leather jackets. Defensively layered, even in summer. She was almost totally wrapped up now too, making those little glimpses of the soles of her feet even more alluring, tempting to run my fingers across that skin. Was she ticklish? I wanted to know, but now was not the time. I sat down next to her, not too close, but the sofa rolled us together and I jogged her and she almost spilled her beer. I apologised, laughing, and then turned to sit cross-legged,

111

perpendicular to Cass.

"The park's not the same without you and Hobbes. That woman with the Pomeranian really just doesn't cut it when it comes to making jokes about Cerberus, you know. Or for talking about funny break-ups of Homerian proportions." I peered at Cass over the top of my glass and saw a quick glance in my direction as I said 'break-ups.' I carried on, "And Jupiter, well, he's never been the best for post-break-up banter. He's far too serious, clearly." Jupiter and Hobbes were currently attached at the face on the floor, both dogs with their rumps raised high, tails wagging. They growled and muttered happily, glad to be reunited.

Cass shuffled slightly and mumbled, "So, er, things went badly with the barista?" She briefly made eye contact and then shoved her nose into her glass, gulping down some beer. Perhaps my suspicions had been right after all. Maybe she was interested in Hanna and was annoyed at me for hooking up with her. Well, maybe we could be friends again now, without any more awkwardness.

"Not badly, as such. Just, well, let's just say that someone realised that they were actually into someone else and that our thing was but a brief dalliance on the path to glorious love. Or something." I clinked my glass into Cass's and she turned and smiled at me, genuinely this time. "Here's to break-ups!" I laughed and we drank.

"So is everything cool with the two of you?" Cass asked.

"Do you mean: Are we safe to hang out at Our Town?" I said, grinning at Cass.

"Maybe."

"Yeah. It's totally fine. It was mutual and I've seen her a bunch of times since as friends. It's pretty nice to have a civilised break-up actually. After Janice and all."

"Cool. And, you know, I am sorry about that night

at the Cobalt. And for being a dick in the park. I'd seen you guys and then a friend gave me some coke and I was just wasted and kind of pissed off, you know? It's not because, well... I'm just a dick like that I guess."

"You were really scary Cass. Like, really scary. It freaked me out and messed things up with Hanna, not that that matters now. But, still, friends don't do that shit. Friends are supposed to protect you from that shit." I put my hand on Cass's knee and she looked up at me. "I don't think you're a dick. OK? But please don't do dick things like taking coke and scaring the shit out of me. We can't be friends if you pull that kind of crap. Seriously."

Cass blinked and I wondered if she was close to crying. The light reflecting in her glasses made it a little difficult to tell. She spoke quietly, saying, "I promise. I'm calming down and figuring my shit out. Honestly. It's long overdue. I'm sorry you got caught up in it. Buds?" Cass put out a bro-fist and I gave her a little bump then pulled her in for a hug. She was more vulnerable right now than I had ever seen her. I could learn to love this gentler, self-aware Cass, I thought, but quickly reminded myself that I had sworn off dating, that I was being career-focused.

"Apology accepted," I said, "And, I will also accept more beer." I held out my glass and Cass rolled her eyes.

"Whisky and Scrabble?" she asked as she got up to retrieve the growler. "Double points for kinky words?"

"Sure!" I was happy that Cass was back on board.

"I'm glad it's safe to hang out at the coffee shop again. I missed that place."

"It was never not safe!"

"For you maybe," Cass said, with her back turned. "Now I'm looking forward to resuming my coffee-drinking position under our favourite barista's unbridled guidance."

I was quite amused that Cass was so quick to want

to see Hanna and I wondered if my earlier comment had made her think that Hanna was interested in her. I couldn't let her know it was actually Em that Hanna was lusting after, but Cass's studious silences had the same effect as Em's gentle questioning, letting me pour out thoughts half-formed and unintended.

Cass handed me my beer and went to dig out the Scrabble board. I would've helped but both dogs had just jumped up onto the couch and decided to use me as a sleeping pad, a head on each of my knees, tuckered out by all that growling and getting reacquainted.

CHAPTER SIXTEEN

I stood in the middle of my living room, trying to remember if I'd packed bug spray when the sound of a car horn interrupted me and caused Jupiter to leap up and run out onto the balcony. I looked out and saw Cass emerge from the Subaru and head to the door of my building. Even from here I could tell that the car was already bursting with stuff. I was doubtful that there'd be space for me, Jupiter, and all our things as part of the group of four people, three dogs, and an awful lot of beer heading to Salt Spring for a couple of days of camping.

I had filled almost a whole backpack with stuff for Jupiter, and now I looked at him accusingly. "Why can't you be a Chihuahua or, I dunno, hunt your own vegan dog kibble or something?" He was too busy pacing back and forth to pay any attention to me though, and Cass's knock on my front door sent him into a tailspin.

Jupiter leapt at Cass as she walked in and I couldn't tell if she yelled "Woah!" because of him or the pile of stuff I'd amassed for the trip. It soon became clear it was

115

because of the latter, and she exclaimed again, "What the fuck, dude? What. The. Fuck." Cass started rummaging through the things as I tried to explain why I needed them all. "We don't need two picnic blankets. Or this huge camping stove. Or, is this a box of paints?"

"Ugh, I thought I might get a chance to sketch?" I said, optimistically.

"You won't," Cass said and pushed the box aside with her foot. "The only sketchy thing happening this weekend will be some drunken skinny dipping." She grinned without looking at me, "If you're lucky." Cass picked up the bungeed-together jumble of tent, Thermarest, and sleeping bags (mine and Jupiter's) and hitched the lot over her shoulder, then hoisted the bag of food up and tucked it under the same arm. With her free hand she carefully picked up the cooler of beers, then said, "Get the door will ya. Precious cargo here."

I held the door open and Jupiter followed her down to the elevator as I scrambled to get my bag and the food hamper. I decided not to take the bag of books I'd planned on finding some quiet time to read. This weekend was going to be anything but quiet it seemed.

As we got to the car, Jupiter and Hobbes greeted each other exuberantly before a vicious sounding Weimeraner popped his head up and scared the bejeebers out of me. This must be Rufus, Cass's friend's dog. Jupiter retreated and Madison got hold of her dog and told him to play nice. Unfortunately, Jupiter decided he wasn't going anywhere near Rufus and ran around to the front of the car where he climbed in on top of Madison's girlfriend, who was not too pleased to suddenly have a seventy-five pound lap dog drooling on her anxiously.

I called my dog over as I put our stuff in the already over-packed trunk. Jupiter ignored my prompts to get in the back with the other dogs and so Cass and I eventually

116

lifted him into the car in a rather undignified fashion. He took up position on the opposite side to Rufus, with Hobbes as a diminutive referee between the two. I worried that Hobbes would get crushed by the two beasts who looked giant in comparison to his twenty pounds or so. I suggested he sat up front with us but Cass said, "Nah, he just bites the gearstick. And he can't read maps for shit."

Leaving the dogs to fight their battles, I climbed into the backseat with Cass, another cooler between us and a bunch of growlers tucked around our feet. The dogs figured out a safe way to stand amidst the camping gear in the back as Madison lurched the car forward and whooped, crying, "Road Trip!"

As we pulled out onto Twelfth Avenue, Madison and her girlfriend, Lindsay, screamed along to the Pixies. I looked over and smiled at Cass as she said, "I warned you. We're a rowdy bunch."

We waited in line at the ferry terminal for half an hour, during which time Cass and Madison smoked three cigarettes each and had a beer. It hadn't yet turned 10am and Lindsay had a seriously sour look on her face. I offered her a beer as I took one from the cooler but she declined, saying, in a deliberately mysterious fashion, "I can't drink at the moment."

"Ah, probation?" I said, jokingly, trying to lighten the mood. She turned and looked at me, horrified.

"No! God. I'm, we're, well. I shouldn't say."

"It's expensive though, right? Like $1500 a pop?" Now Lindsay turned around and looked at me properly for the first time. I think she was trying to figure out how I knew.

"Did Cass say something?"

"Nope. Just, there are few reasons why people don't drink 'at the moment,' and getting knocked up is one. Or,

117

I guess, Candida, but you've already eaten a packet of Skittles so I'm pretty sure that's not it."

I'd like to think that Lindsay looked impressed at my detective skills but she was one of those people that appeared to have resting bitch face, so I really couldn't tell.

"Yeah. Well, we weren't telling people," she said. "It's the third try and if it doesn't work this time then it's probably not going to happen."

"That's why your missus is drinking already then, huh? The stress of impending parenthood?"

"Something like that." Lindsay slumped back in her chair, facing away from me again. "This is supposed to be a relaxing weekend so that I'm more likely to conceive at the appointment next week but I swear if she's carousing all the time I'm not even going to go to the clinic."

I was silent for a moment, thinking about the stress of IVF and how Madison must feel pretty ineffectual, while Lindsay was clearly highly anxious. "I'm sorry it's so tough. But, one day I might be calling on you guys to help calm me down if I take that route." I smiled at the back of her head, thinking that babies were still some way off, thank god. "I hope it works out for you. Maybe Madison's just trying to help by drinking all the booze so you don't accidentally have any."

Lindsay snorted and offered me a Skittle, which I declined as I couldn't remember if these were the candy that had ground-up bugs or gelatin in the crunchy coating. As I tried to remember, Madison got back into the car, downed her beer and handed the empty to Cass to return to the cooler. The cars ahead were starting to be waved onto the ferry and as we began rolling forward Cass whooped along with Madison, then turned to me, eyebrows raised and said, "What? Too cool for a little whoop?"

118

"Just too sober," I said, tossing back my own beer and stashing it in the cooler as we headed over the ramp and into the dark belly of the *Queen of Nanaimo*.

Lindsay wanted to stay in the car with the dogs but the rest of us went out onto the deck to watch Vancouver disappear across the Georgia Straight. Cass and Madison passed Cass's hip flask back and forth and I decided that either myself or Lindsay should drive us to the campsite once we arrived on Salt Spring Island.

After a little while the sun emerged from behind the lone cloud in the sky. The three of us walked over to one of the vacant lifejacket chests and spread out, using our sweaters as pillows now it was too hot to wear them. With Cass's check shirt, Madison's short shorts and white shirt, and my new Aviators, I imagined that we looked like a loungy vintage Tommy Hilfiger ad. If Em were here she'd think up some witty slogan and sell us our own images.

The sun was deliciously warm on my exposed skin, so I unbuttoned my shirt a little to extend the sensation. A calm silence enveloped our trio, interrupted only by the sound of scampering children as they hurried past the tableau, playing hide and seek up and down the metal decks and clanging steps.

The combination of beer, sunshine, and early morning packing panic pushed me into drowsiness and I let my mind swim a little to the soft crash of the waves and the languorous roll of the ferry.

Next to me, Cass let her arms drop to her sides, her palms facing upwards, her thumb gently grazing the skin on my wrist. I felt the heat rise in my neck, up my throat, and the familiar pressure of lust between my legs. Cass's thumb was making tiny, almost imperceptible movements across my skin, small enough to be the slow twitch of sleep or the rocking of the boat but enough to

119

set my body throbbing. I allowed the feeling to continue, enjoying how my nerves lit up with even this tiny stimulus. I imagined that Cass and I were alone, that the ferry had been abandoned by all but the two of us, that she was on top of me, her thumb working its soft caress down my belly, her lips on my collarbone, those plump pink lips with the clear central line and that sharp notch at the top, her tongue slipping into my mouth, wet and waiting for her.

"Coffee?"

"Huh?"

Madison pulled me back to reality, and Cass too it seemed as we both jolted upright, almost banging heads. "Huh?" we both said again and I looked down at Cass's hand, the skin appearing a little bluer than usual due to the sun's lingering effect on my vision.

"Sure, I could use some coffee," Cass said, and swung her legs off the bench. I blinked myself out of my reverie, and she asked, "Are you coming?"

I nodded, wondering if this was what the whole weekend would be like, with me adrift on a soft wave of lust.

"I'm going to get Lindsay a coffee," Madison said. "Then I'll relieve her of dog-sitting duty so she can get some sun. I hear vitamin D's good for making babies or something, and it's sure cheaper than all those drugs."

Cass laughed and I smiled, sensing the defeat in Madison's voice. She was older than Lindsay and I imagined she had resigned herself some time ago to not being a biological parent. It was clearly tough going through that disappointment again with her younger partner.

"I'm sorry it's not working out for you guys," Cass said. "When it's my turn I guess I'll just get some dude drunk and steal his sperm, right?"

"Eurgh. Seriously Cass, don't. Anyway, you repel

120

men. You know it," Madison said, laughing.

I couldn't resist asking Cass, "I didn't know you wanted kids?"

"Yeah, someday. Just with the right person, you know." She was still drowsy enough not to be her usual defensive self.

I was surprised though when Madison smiled at me and said, "Cass is looking for the whole white picket fence thing. Right? Marriage, kids, a little buddy for Hobbes. Just a shame she can't keep her strap on in her pants long enough to find Mrs. Right, right?" She laughed at Cass who was now awake enough to kick her in the butt. Still, she didn't disagree and avoided my eyes as she held the heavy door open to get us back inside and on our way to coffee.

As we waited in the car to off-load from the ferry, Madison fell asleep on Lindsay's shoulder and snored loud day-drunk snores. I drove us off slowly and navigated the winding roads of Salt Spring Island. The Rainbow Road site was only about fifteen minutes from the ferry though, so Madison soon had to wake up from her power nap and wipe the drool off her girlfriend's jacket.

We all piled out of the car and the dogs stretched out and sniffed their new surroundings. Jupiter was in his element. Cass headed over to the office to find out which site we were booked into, and I started unloading things from the car. Jupiter dashed in and out of the trees nearby and when he went a little too far for my liking I whistled him back. As he started towards me he was startled by the sound of a tent being unzipped, so instead of coming back to me he turned and ran full tilt at the emerging camper.

I dropped the tents and ran over to rescue whoever was about to get slobbered on. Happily, I found that I

121

had come to the rescue of, quite possibly, the most beautiful woman I had ever seen. She was wearing a loosely knit white dress, which I could just imagine Jupiter getting completely tangled in as he jumped at her. I prepared to be mightily embarrassed, but before I got to them the woman had already crouched down and asked my dog to sit. He did so happily and was enjoying head-pats and ear scratches as I blundered over to apologise.

"Hi! Sorry!" I said, breathlessly, and went to grab Jupiter's collar.

"No problem. It's nice to see such a happy camper!" The woman stood up and extended her hand, which was bedecked with rings and hennaed on both sides. "Celeste. Nice to meet you."

"Kate. Happy to meet you."

"Here for the weekend?"

"Yup. You?"

"Oh, just passing through. I have a show in town tonight. You and your friends should come." She smiled and looked over my shoulder at Lindsay and Madison who were gawping at us.

"Sure, I don't think we have plans yet. Where and when?"

Celeste reached into a crocheted bag hanging from a nearby tree and retrieved a flier. It was styled like a tarot card but had a picture of Celeste standing like a tree in the centre, the band name, *Jupiter Rising*, circling her head and hands. I laughed and then realised how that might seem rude.

"Sorry, it's just that my dog is called Jupiter."

"Oh! How sweet. Well, he should come too."

"I'm pretty sure he's underage so that might not work out too well. Thanks though." I stood grinning at her, wondering how to wrestle my dog away from his new friend.

122

"Well, I'll let you get set up. See you later!" Celeste zipped up her tent and swung the bag over her shoulder, heading off into the woods.

As I returned to Lindsay and Madison, I saw Cass had joined them and was asking what they were staring at.

Madison laughed. "You missed out. Kate got in first, thanks to Jupiter."

"Missed out on what?"

"Only the hottest woman alive," Madison said and Lindsay elbowed her. "What!? You were leering too, don't deny it." She turned to me and asked, "Did you get her number? What did she give you?"

I could feel myself blushing and held out the flier. "Not sure if it'll be any good but..."

"We should totally go! You're single, right? Island fling potential!" Madison handed the flier to Cass.

Lindsay picked up their tent and told Madison to stop living vicariously.

"Just living, baby, just living!" Madison made a start towards our site and Cass handed the flier back to me.

"If you guys want to go then I can stay here with the dogs, no problem," Cass said while picking up some gear and walking off.

"What? No. That's cool." I rushed after Cass and tried to take my tent from her but she shook me off and carried on up the trail, leaving me to wonder what her problem was.

When I got to the site I worked in silence alongside Lindsay and Cass, who were setting up their tents. Madison went back and forth fetching things from the car in order to prepare lunch. The dogs ran around and got themselves tangled in guy ropes before losing interest and going to chew the grass near our site. They were pretty happy to no longer be stuck in the car on a noisy and scary ferry.

I looked over at Cass, hoping to make conversation but she had her head down and was violently hammering in tent pegs, cursing as they bent and skipped out of the hard ground. It hadn't rained for a few days and there were roots all over the site, making it tricky to get the pegs into the earth at any depth to secure the lines.

"Maybe you can just tie the guys round some heavy rocks," I said, trying to be helpful. She didn't even look up so I stayed quiet until my own tent was up and I'd arranged the sleeping pad and bags inside for myself and Jupiter. Knowing the drill, Jupes promptly skipped into the tent and fell asleep across both bags. I had a feeling I'd be little spoon later.

"Lunch bell! Lunch bell!" Madison called as she rang a bear bell in each fist.

Lindsay and I came running, hungry for veggie burgers with all the trimmings. Cass carried on setting up stuff inside her tent. When I got up to go and drag her over, Madison put her hand on my arm and told me not to. "She's being a moody fuck so best to leave her be."

"Why? What's up?" I asked.

Lindsay rolled her eyes as Madison whispered, "She's given up weed and sex. God knows why."

"She's trying to figure things out, that's all," Lindsay said. "Some people do that, you know. Instead of relying on chemical props."

"Sex isn't a chemical," Madison said.

"Well, it may as well be for Cass. If she goes a week without getting laid then she's in withdrawal."

I ate my burger in silence, unsure as to whether Cass could hear us or not.

"If she gets unbearable then I'll slip some Xanax in her beer," Madison laughed and then, as Lindsay and I stared at her in horror, she quickly added, "I'm joking! Obviously I wouldn't do that!"

Cass emerged from her tent and made up a

sandwich, piling on a little of everything so that the thing was a behemoth that would never fit in her mouth. She squashed it down, its contents oozing out onto the plastic plate.

"I'm going for a walk. I'll pick up beer and see you back here later. K?" It wasn't a question as Cass took off into the woods, turning slightly to yell thanks for lunch.

"Moody fuck," Madison said, and I worried about how the afternoon would look now I'd been left with two people I barely knew, playing third wheel, with three dogs to manage. I looked around and saw that Rufus was asleep in the sun at Madison's feet, Jupiter was still in the tent, and Hobbes was staring at our sandwiches, drooling profusely. Cass whistled from somewhere in the trees and he took one lingering look at my lunch before heading after her.

"Anyone fancy a swim after lunch?" Lindsay asked. "We could drive down to the lake. God knows I need some sun."

"You guys go," I said. "I'll stay here with the dogs if you like."

Madison shushed me and insisted that I had earned a swim. "And, don't forget, Kate, we might run into your potential fling!"

CHAPTER SEVENTEEN

Within an hour, the three of us and the dogs were at the lake. We found a pretty quiet stretch and tied the dogs to a tree so they couldn't harass any fleshy, nude sunbathers.

We stripped off and slipped into the water, which was horribly cold despite the warmth of the day. Lindsay had shucked off all her clothes, while Madison and I had stuck to shorts and shirts. As I came back out of the water after my swim I spotted Celeste towelling herself off about twenty feet away. She saw me and waved, her long hair running down over her breasts, the wildness of her bush glistening in the sun. Her body shimmered as she walked towards me.

"Hey! Isn't it gorgeous? I love this lake. I always come here when I'm on the island. Can I sit?" She didn't wait for an answer, but just squeezed in next to me on my towel, still naked, her clothes nowhere to be seen. I looked straight ahead at Madison and Lindsay who were ducking each other in the water.

"So, you're a musician, huh?" I asked, figuring I should make conversation with this naked stranger.

126

"Yeah. I love to play. How about you? Maybe we can jam later?" She was staring at me, her knees hugged to her chest, head swivelled. If I turned our faces would almost be touching.

"I, er, I don't really play anything. I'm not very creative that way."

"Oh, psh. I think everyone's creative. You probably write or paint or something, yeah?"

"Well, I suppose. I do paint and I do web design and stuff so there's some artistry to that I guess."

I turned and smiled at her and she grinned, her teeth perfectly aligned and her eyes a fantastic light blue. There were freckles all across the bridge of her nose, as if she'd already had her fill of sun for the year, despite the earliness of the season.

"You ever tried to play anything?"

I turned away and said, "Sure. I have a guitar, I just suck at it."

"Do you practice?"

"Nope!" I laughed and said, "I know I should but I always seem to be doing something else. I guess it's just not a priority."

"What are your priorities then?" She asked, seriously.

"Oh, the usual. Finding a nice lady to U-Haul with, marry and have two kids to successfully replace ourselves in the world." I smiled and then said, "No, wait. I mean getting drunk and getting laid. Yeah. That."

"Those are pretty different things," Celeste said, still being serious.

"Well, yeah. I was joking."

"Oh?" Celeste started at me and I looked away again. This woman was alarmingly literally minded, especially for a musical hippy who sat next to strangers in the nude. I felt a little unnerved. Perhaps she had seen through the joke and recognised that, actually, I did want

127

all those things. Maybe this is why you shouldn't talk to strangers, particularly naked ones; they ask annoyingly insightful questions, not knowing how to dodge the landmines in your banter.

Madison and Lindsay were heading back from the water and looked a little surprised to find me all cosy with Celeste. They introduced themselves and offered Celeste a beer.

"Oh, I don't drink. Thanks. I've got some weed though, if anyone wants in?"

Madison looked at Lindsay who shrugged her shoulders and said, "Go ahead."

The two of them moved over to where Celeste had left her stuff and Lindsay dried off and pulled on some clothes, the sun having retreated behind a cloud.

We sat in silence for a while, and then Lindsay got out a book and propped herself against the tree to read. Madison and Celeste were smoking nearby and the occasional waft of their joint reached us, causing Lindsay to look up sternly. I decided to take Jupiter for a walk, announcing the plan and unhooking his leash from around the tree.

We sauntered out into the forest and I pushed my sunglasses up onto my head, marveling at the glorious light filtering through the cathedral of tall spruce. We had been walking for barely ten minutes when Hobbes careered out of the bushes straight at Jupiter, scaring the shit out of me.

Cass emerged on the trail up ahead a couple of minutes later and smiled broadly. I guessed that her bad mood had lifted as she asked, "'Sup?"

"Hey. Did you walk all the way from the campsite?"

"Yeah. Needed to clear my head a bit, you know." She fell into step behind me as I turned to go back to the lake. "Did you get first prize?" Cass asked, then laughed at my puzzled response. "In the wet t-shirt contest."

128

"Oh! Ha. No. I think that went to Lindsay for having no t-shirt." Cass smiled, but the smile quickly evaporated as I said, "Or to Celeste maybe."

"Oh, you guys went to the lake with the woman from the site?"

"No. She was just there. Her and Madison were just smoking a joint. I got a bit bored."

"Good job you ran into me then." Cass's smile had returned and she elbowed me in the side, laughing. "C'mon, race ya back to the lake. Last one in's a dirty hipster!"

I chased Cass, and the dogs bounded along beside us. I dropped my bag as we passed by Lindsay and we all headed out into the water. Cass had flung off a couple of layers of clothing and was down to her bra and shorts as she dove into the lake. I leapt in after her, the shock of the cold water hitting me once again. Jupiter barked at the edge of the water and little Hobbes was jauntily swimming out to Cass, his nose lifted up high.

I reached out a hand to splash Cass with water but she got me first and I choked and laughed, splashing her back. She dived under and I followed suit, wary of her stealing my shorts from beneath me. Sure enough, she had started tugging at them and I slapped her hands away, trying to keep my mouth closed so I didn't swallow any more lake water.

We both resurfaced, our faces almost touching. The water shone on Cass's eyelashes, giving her the appearance of a diamond encrusted drag queen, just for a second before she wiped her hands across her face, flicking the wet hair from her eyes. She grabbed my hand and tipped herself onto her back, calling "Make like an otter won't you." I turned to float on my back too and we bobbed around in circles for a while, holding onto each other, gently paddling with our free hands and bumping into each other every so often. I closed my eyes

129

and felt the wonderful weightlessness of my body, and the cool grip of Cass's hand in mine. She relaxed her grip for a second and played out our fingers until they were only just touching, then pulled me back in again, laughing happily.

As we bumped into each other softly, I asked Cass "When were you the most happy you've ever been?" I was prepared to wait a while for the answer, having just let the question sneak out of me without too much thought.

She sighed quietly and placed her palm against mine before entwining our fingers again.

Still, I waited. Cass sighed again, then said, "Now. I think I'm most happy now."

I was quiet for a moment before asking, "With me?"

Almost imperceptibly, Cass murmured in agreement. I smiled and closed my eyes again, savouring the moment.

Cass was also silent for a minute, then she paddled around me and reached for my other hand. Slowly, Cass traced her fingers across the palm of my left hand, stopping only one she felt the ridge of the ring on my finger. I had found the silver band a few days ago and, without really thinking about it, had slid the engagement ring back onto my finger and forgotten to take it off.

Cass was playing with the ring now, as I thought about how it had taken me six months or so to take the damn thing off after Janice left, and the ease with which I now wore it again as if it were nothing more than jewellery. Cass let go of my hand and quickly swam away, showering me with water as she headed for the beach.

I sat up in the water and stared after her, watching as she waded through the shallow water, her shorts sticking to her thighs, the bones of her back catching the sun as she bent to retrieve the clothes she'd dropped on her rush to the lake. She walked toward Madison and

Lindsay, and I saw them point at Celeste, prostrate on her towel close by. As Cass moved toward Celeste, I started swimming back, but by the time I had climbed out Cass and Celeste had packed up and headed into the trees.

"Where'd Cass go?" I asked Madison and Lindsay, breathless.

"Oh, she decided she needed a smoke. I guess they headed back to camp. We were thinking of going too, if you're done swimming?" Lindsay said. They were propped up against each other, reading magazines and petting Jupiter and Rufus, now best buds, nose to nose across their laps.

"Yeah. I'm ready," I said, wondering what had gotten into Cass, and then thinking how good it would be to crack a beer right about now.

Cass and Celeste weren't there when we got back to the campsite, but Hobbes was asleep in Madison's car.

We set about making dinner, saving enough for Cass should she return. She didn't, and the sun sank lower and lower until Madison asked if I wanted to go to Celeste's gig in town.

"I don't know. Maybe."

"Well, we could just look in and if it's crap then we can always grab beer at the liquor store and head back here for some stargazing." Madison smiled at Lindsay and wrapped her arm around her girlfriend's shoulder. I was wary of ending up spending the evening alone in my tent trying not to hear sex noises. I hoped they weren't squealers, and was glad I'd packed the earplugs. Jupiter would just have to suffer. It would be embarrassing if he howled though.

We set out to walk into town, headlamps ready for the dark walk home later. Hobbes and Rufus were asleep in the car and Jupiter was snoozing in my tent, his head under the pile of sleeping bags where he was snoring happily, exhausted from running up and down the lake edge while I swam.

When we arrived at the pub there was no sign yet of Celeste. The guy strumming his guitar and wailing plaintively was a bit too much to bear so we went to the liquor store and picked out a local heather ale and a couple of porters. Madison texted Cass; I didn't seem to have cell coverage on the island. We'd left food out for her at the site and I was a bit worried some chipmunks would get into it while we were away.

Down by the water, we piled onto a bench and Madison and I passed a bottle between us. It was starting to get cold so I pulled on another sweater and waited for the beer jacket to kick in.

After a while we spotted Celeste heading down the pier, a guitar slung over her shoulder. She looked really high and I wondered how she was going to be able to play. She called us over and we followed her back into the bar. I drained the last of the ale on the way in, and Madison slapped me on the back and laughed.

A few minutes later, Celeste was up on the stage, suddenly appearing totally sober and professional. She played beautifully, her voice taking on an unusual, flighty and tremulous quality, but with an underlying strength. Halfway through the third song she looked up and scanned the audience, her gaze stopping at the door and a broad smile appearing on her face. I turned and saw that Cass was leaning on the wall at the back of the room, having just walked in with a guitar hanging across her chest.

Celeste waggled her finger and announced a guest star for the evening and five seconds later Cass was on stage. Madison and Lindsay and I all gaped at Cass and then each other as the two women sang and played and,

132

in Cass's case, drank a lot of beer before leaving the stage to a hail of applause. Cass took a bow and headed to the bar, her arm over Celeste's shoulder, not even a glance in our direction.

"Break one rule, break 'em all, eh?" Madison said and headed to the bar to get us drinks and see what Cass was up to. I wasn't sure if the nausea I felt was due to too much sun, too much beer, or the sight of Cass and Celeste suddenly being so intimate.

Lindsay was peering at me oddly and seemed about to say something but then closed her mouth and busied herself looking for something in her bag.

Madison returned with beers but didn't say anything about her chat with Cass. "Apparently, the next guy to play sounds like Johnny Cash. I can't decide if that will be awesome or terrible, but I'm erring towards terrible," Madison said.

I thanked her for the beer and asked if they wanted to stick around.

"Sure. May as well see what the local talent is like, eh?"

I drank my beer and concentrated on the stage, willing myself not to look over to see what Cass and Celeste were up to. After a while of listening to the faux Mr. Cash I went to get a round of beers, knowing I was heading towards tipsiness but no longer caring. Cass and her new friend were nowhere to be seen.

The night turned to open mic and we sat through a couple of terribly angsty numbers before a great harmonica player wowed the crowd. Soon, though, I began to feel the room starting to spin a little and so I told Madison and Lindsay I was heading back. As I left, I dug around in my bag for the head lamp and tried to appear a little less drunk than I suddenly felt. Madison and Lindsay offered to come with me but I told them to stay, needing the quietness of the walk back to think, or

133

to throw up, depending on how things went.

After walking away from the bar I recognised the road back up to the woods and soon found the entrance to the Mouat Trail. This would lead me back to the camp site, and I paused for a second to turn on my head lamp. I felt a little foolish for having gotten more tipsy than intended, and then felt even more foolish as, after a couple of steps into the forest, I stumbled over a root and hit my head on a low-lying branch. Taking a breath, I tried to calm my nerves and quell the nausea rising in my throat; part anxiety, part booze.

As I walked back to the site, I heard the occasional pinging sound of nighttime disc golfers hitting their target. They were doing surprisingly well given the lack of moonlight penetrating through the trees. I stopped again, having walked into a giant cobweb. I felt trapped, stifled in the creepy woods and, suddenly, completely overwhelmed with sadness. For a minute or two I let the despair wash over me. Then I thought about going and getting Jupiter and packing up my tent and retreating to the Salt Spring Inn for the night. I'd hitch a ride to the ferry in the morning and could be home by midday. I really did not want to spend the night in close proximity to Celeste's tent. Two sheets of canvas were not enough to separate me from the inevitable sounds of Cass and Celeste fucking.

When I got back to camp I saw that the food had gone from the picnic table, but there was no light in Cass's tent, or in Celeste's. I unzipped my tent and let Jupiter out to pee. He immediately ran over to Celeste's tent and I whispered for him to come back. Eventually, he got the message, peed on a nearby tree and then ran over to herd me into my own tent. As I climbed in I realised I was too tired to go through with my plan to decamp. Jupiter snuggled up next to me and I turned out

134

the lantern hanging above my head.

A few minutes later, as I was falling asleep I hear a stifled laugh from what I presumed was Celeste's tent. A light flickered on nearby and I shifted Jupiter aside so I could undo the mesh on my tent door and peer out into the night. I watched the shadows dance across Celeste's tent. Two bodies moving together. Then the light went out again and there was more laughter, then gasping.

I dug around in the darkness to find my earplugs and then crawled back into my sleeping bag. I did not want my dreams to be mired by the sounds of Cass and Celeste getting it on. I hugged Jupiter tight and cried as quietly as I could into his neck, letting him lick my face clean as we both drifted into a troubled sleep.

CHAPTER EIGHTEEN

I watched the wake of a False Creek ferry dissipate against the wall beneath my dangling legs, while I waited for Janice to arrive. We had arranged to meet for a drink and so I was sitting by the water with a growler of Brassneck's *Identity Crisis* stowed in my bag alongside some Mason jars.

I'd arrived early, not wanting to turn up rushed and sweaty. Now, however, I realised that this simply gave me time to build up my anxiety. There's something to be said for arriving perfectly on time, which Janice did.

We hugged and Janice held me a little longer than anticipated. She was using different shampoo, something with papaya. I felt my throat closing a little and was keen to start drinking. After getting back from the island trip, I'd texted Janice to see if she wanted to meet up. I had been angry at Cass for leaving a day early to drive around with Celeste. She had left me with her friends and had given us no idea where she was. I figured she'd be back in the city now as she had work and , but who knew with Cass. Maybe she was on a tour with her new beau.

Perhaps being angry and sad wasn't the best reason to get in touch with Janice and arrange to catch up, but I had wanted a drinking buddy, preferably someone familiar.

Janice suggested we took a walk and after a little while she took my hand and pulled me through some trees to a little hidden spot on the seawall. We swung our legs out to rest on the sloping cobblestones and I took the beer out of my bag and handed it to Janice.

She held the growler, almost reverently and then took a deep breath and asked, "How are you Kate?"

I paused, the jars ready in my hands, and returned her gaze for second. I had been tempted to answer glibly but instead had waited, smiled at her and said calmly, "I'm doing OK. Better."

Janice patted my hand in an oddly maternal fashion and nodded. She unscrewed the top of the growler as she looked out over the water at downtown. "Things change so quickly sometimes," she said, and I wasn't sure if she meant the skyline or something else. "I think I did a lot of growing while I was away. I think I needed that." She poured out the beer, and then took my hand again and said, "I wasn't good to you in the end, and I'm sorry. I was just very sad that things didn't seem right anymore and I wasn't sure how to tell you any of that. I'm sorry it's taken me this long to get to this point." She carried on staring at me, her face relaxed and happy, sincere.

"Thank you. That's good to hear," I said, wondering how much growing I'd done while Janice had been away. "I think I'm still a bit confused by it all to be honest. I still..." I was going to say I still didn't really understand but it seemed rather academic now. We were moving on and being friends and maybe in time I'd figure out where things had gone wrong in our relationship but just asking outright didn't seem necessary any more.

Janice let go of my hand and asked quietly, "You

still?"

I laughed and waved away the question. "Nothing, it doesn't matter. How's your drink?" I sipped my beer as Janice murmured appreciation. We watched in silence as a couple of paddleboarders went by, the first considerably more accomplished than the second. This guy was less poised but determined to stay upright and as we watched his progress I asked Janice, "What was the weirdest thing, no… the most fun thing you did while you were travelling?"

She looked up and thought about it for a second or two. "Honestly, I think it was watching an olive tree be tickled." She laughed as I looked at her quizzically. "There are these machines that get launched up into the trees and they have, like, a bazillion fingers that literally tickle the olives off of the tree to fall on the sheets they've laid out below." She paused, taking a sip of her beer. Then she looked out across the water and said, "If you listen really quietly you can hear the tree laughing."

I elbowed her lightly and said, "Shut up!" Then I asked, "They seriously tickle the tree?"

"Yes! They let me have a go. This family I stayed with in Greece had an olive farm, or kind of an olive farm anyway, and I was there just at the right time and so I helped out. It was amazing! Less messy than crushing grapes with my feet in Italy."

"You really did that? Fuck. Like, while wearing a white dress and looking fabulous with lots of hot Italian ladies?"

"Actually, no, that was a lie. I wish!" Janice filled up our glasses and raised a toast. "To old friends and new friends and bold friends and true friends."

"Hear hear."

"How about we blow this joint and I show you my new pad? There's someone I want you to meet," Janice said mysteriously.

"Did you get a cat?"

"Shhh. You'll spoil the surprise." Janice touched her finger to my lips and I wondered if she was already a little tipsy after just two glasses of beer. Had she eaten today? She always used to forget to eat and she was looking pretty waif-like these days. I decided I'd make us something when we got back to her place.

As we were walking to Janice's apartment, we passed a Subway, so I pretended I was hungry and lured her in to load her up with a foot-long sandwich, complete with avocado slices and vegan patty. Although I appreciated the hygiene of people wearing gloves while shoving salad and pickles into a ciabatta, somehow it always turned my stomach. I guess I like my food served with love, rather than a fear of disease. The sterile cloudy white gloves make it feel less like food and more like fuel but I suppose in this case I was just hoping to get Janice to eat something.

As she devoured her sandwich, she mumbled, "This was a great idea!" Sauce was dripping down her chin and I watched as a slice of tomato tried to make a break for freedom and then got lodged in a twist of her scarf. I handed her a napkin and shoved some chips in my mouth as we walked up the hill to her new place.

Janice demolished the food and was done by the time we got to her apartment building, where she rummaged for her key fob and used it to activate the development's sophisticated entry system. I admired the shiny efficiency while thinking of how often my own stubborn, half-assed buzzer intercom failed. For a second I entertained the thoughts of moving somewhere better, realising that I could actually afford it now. I kind of liked the charm of my slightly decrepit abode though, and, anyway, I really couldn't face boxing things up again and dealing with Jupiter's pre and post-move jitters. He typically turned psychotic whenever he saw packing tape and things disappearing into neatly stacked Frogboxes.

We walked through a cobbled courtyard, complete with some incipient palm trees. I imagined Janice must have been feeling the European influence when she picked out her apartment. She held the door open for me and then quickly told me to close my eyes and stay put as she scampered down the hallway. I removed my shoes blindly, thinking that maybe Janice had adopted a snake and was about to wrap it around my neck and yell, "Surprise! Meet Barry the boa!" I prayed that this condo strata had rules against reptiles.

Janice returned and told me to put out my hands. I braced myself for the cool dryness of scales, or the fluffy weight of a kitten. Instead, she placed something boxlike in my hands and when I opened my eyes I saw myself staring back at me. "Oh!" I mustered a shocked utterance as I examined the painting. It was undoubtedly me, and I was pretty impressed by the skill of the artist. I looked up at Janice and asked, "Did you?"

"Yep! I took painting classes for a while in Italy and I was thinking a lot about you, trying to work things out, you know." She was leaning against the hallway wall, her hands behind her back and her head down but eyes raised to try to judge how I felt about the picture.

"It's really good. I'm a bit, well, I'm a bit taken aback at how good it is. And, obviously, it's a bit weird that I like it as it's a picture of me. Which photo did you copy?"

"Oh, I didn't, I found that it's easier to go by memory so I just kept thinking about our trip to Nelson that one time and how beautiful you were just sitting by the river reading *Wind in the Willows* and falling asleep. I think that's one of my happiest memories you know."

I put out a hand to touch her shoulder and thanked her, feeling awash with nostalgia.

"It's yours. If you want it, I mean. Maybe it'd be

140

weird to have a picture of yourself and all but I hope you like it."

My hand was still on her arm and so I pulled her in for a hug and told her I'd love to keep it. Janice mumbled something into my shoulder that sounded like, "I missed you."

I answered with a questioning "Hmm?" as we pulled apart.

"I missed you," she said, but the last word was muffled again as she kissed me, her hand around the back of my neck, her fingers playing into my hair. I could taste the chipotle mayo on her breath and I let her push me back against the opposite wall, her other hand now working at unfastening my belt and loosening my shirt all at the same time. Her skin felt so good against mine, so right after all this time, and the voice in my head just stopped chattering as she pulled me towards her bedroom and on top of her once again.

I slipped the straps of her dress off her shoulders and traced a path back across the body I had loved so earnestly for so long. She felt new, more alive than ever, and the combination of comforting memory and the potential to discover her anew was bewildering. We quickly undressed and I tried to remember the last time we were naked with each other. In the last few months of our relationship we had taken to hiding our bodies beneath the covers, terrified to express desire or to receive anything at all in case, perhaps, it was later held out as a debt of love. Now, though, we explored each other slowly and Janice asked if she could go down on me, producing a dental dam from the bedside cabinet.

We'd never used protection when we were together, having been tested and monogamous thereafter. Somehow it felt exciting and sexy, something I'd never associated with dental dams. It meant that things were different, not boring and safe and the same as before,

141

that we were new people who didn't quite know each other anymore. Nothing brought this home more than the harness Janice wriggled me into later that night, straddling me and making sounds I'd never heard her make before. She'd asked me back to hers to meet someone new and I began to wonder if she had meant herself. This new Janice bore hardly any resemblance to the demure woman I'd been with for so many years.

When we both collapsed, exhausted and sweaty, onto her bed later, I was adamant I wouldn't fall asleep, knowing I had to head home for Jupiter. Janice kissed my shoulder and embraced me as I perched on the edge of her bed, gathering my thoughts and my clothes. I brought her hand to my lips and she asked if I was free for breakfast and, just like that, we were together again and I was lost to myself and the world.

CHAPTER NINETEEN

I awoke tangled in Janice's sheets, her arm draped across my chest and her head buried in the crook of my neck. Jupiter was staring at me from the doorway of the bedroom. I blinked and we looked at each other for a while. Today would be the day we'd go home. This couldn't carry on. I needed a change of clothes, and my own bed, and to not turn up late to work every day this week with a dopey postcoital grin. Janice was murmuring herself awake though, and, as she clutched at my hand and wriggled her body against me, Jupiter sighed and went out to wait in the hallway. Tomorrow, tomorrow I'd go home.

When I woke up again Janice was in the kitchen making tea. I joined her and surveyed the apartment, marvelling at just how much takeout we'd eaten since hooking up. I picked up the harness from the couch and threw it back into the bedroom before sitting down and smiling at Janice as she handed me tea. I needed coffee but Janice wasn't drinking caffeine and we had decided not to be seen in public together, not yet, so breakfast out was out.

"I think I'll go home today." I said, into my mug of tea.

"Cool. I'd love to see your place. I'll come over after work with sushi." She smiled and went to shower, and I wondered if she had simply missed the point or was wilfully overlooking my need for space. Maybe things hadn't changed much after all.

The next morning I was heading out with Jupiter when Janice ran after me, pulling on one of my sweaters as she called for me to wait. "I want to come too! It's been a while since Jupiter and I hung out in the park."

I smiled wanly as she slipped her arm through mine, apparently forgetting that we had decided to keep things secret for now.

Janice was throwing the Frisbee for Jupiter when I spotted Cass across the park. She was heading in our direction but I wasn't sure if she'd actually seen us as she was looking over her shoulder and calling Hobbes. I hadn't run into her for a week or so as I'd been holed up at Janice's with Jupes and we'd been going to Charleston Park every day.

Cass got closer and she nodded at me and smiled. She looked tired. I went to hug her, but Jupiter ran between us, and then Janice was by my side saying she had to leave. She gestured at her phone and rolled her eyes before briefly smiling at Cass. She didn't wait for an introduction, just kissed me and skipped off to work. I closed my eyes and then turned back to Cass, not knowing what to expect.

"Dude. What the fuck?" she said, shoving her hands into her pockets and staring at me wide-eyed.

"Yeah. Um. So that's, er, that's Janice." I raised my eyebrows and smiled hopefully at Cass who stepped back and actually turned around in a circle before walking

144

toward me again. She opened her mouth to say something but then closed it again and just stared at me.

I started talking, saying how we'd gone out for a drink and then had ended up sleeping together and that it had been a weird week or so. Eventually I just trailed off as Cass blinked at me uncomprehendingly.

"You're fucking your ex. That's what you're saying. You're fucking your ex who fucked you over. So that whole 'moving on' thing did nothing for ya, eh?" Cass said with an eerie calm, taking her hands out of her pockets and then wrapping them around herself as if she wasn't sure whether to shake me or hit me or hug me.

"Yeah. It got a bit complicated," I mumbled, feeling incredibly stupid and sad.

"Yeah. Looks like." Cass walked past me and I called after her but she just waved her hands in dismissal. I watched Hobbes break off from playing with Jupiter and follow Cass out of the park. Jupiter stood by my side and looked after her, then looked up at me as if to reflect my own bewilderment. He started after Cass, but then turned to see if I was following. When I didn't, he ambled slowly back to me. He knew I wasn't making the best decisions and so did I.

CHAPTER TWENTY

Marla was the nicest HR person in the world, but, because I barely understood my contract, I always worried when she called me into the office. I was terrified that the company would cut me loose, refuse to pay me, and leave me destitute. Maybe the real sign that you're succeeding as an adult is having job security, by which I mean turning up at your job and not having that nagging fear that every little slip could mean you're out on your ass.

Luckily, when I arrived at the office ten minutes earlier than requested, I saw that Marla was laughing at some joke with my boss, Harrison, and as she called me over he was grinning at me. This must be a good sign. Unless they were both great actors and were lulling me into a false sense of security.

"Kate! Great news!" Harrison said. "We want you to be lead on a new project we just picked up. How would you feel about that? Marla and I were talking about things and we realised that you've basically been heading your own team for a while now, just without the

146

recognition. This new project is right up your alley."
Harrison put his hand on my elbow and was leaning in
close, as if we were conspiring. Unfortunately, any
attempt at subtlety was lost as Harrison's voice boomed
and reverberated around the foam panelled walls. "It's
perfect for you, Kate! Perfect!" he whisper-yelled.

I was a little alarmed at their enthusiasm, wondering
what this incredible project could be that was so ideal for
me. Was it a website about radical knitting dogs
discovering their queer identities? I started imagining the
project brief and then realised that I should pay attention
to the actual project itself.

"I'd be stoked to head up the design team, sure." I
tried to speak calmly but the words felt like treacle in my
mouth. This was a big fucking deal in this company.
Contractors barely ever headed up anything so maybe
this meant they might want to hire me as an employee.
Jeez, maybe I was actually on my way to that job security
and adulthood I had just been thinking about. "So,
what's the project?"

"It's for an NGO, a local one. They make
documentaries and they need a flashy new -" Harrison
kept on talking but I could hardly pay attention. This was
the company Cass worked for. It would be so much fun
working with her! I was excited to let her know,
assuming that she was on the same project of course.
The local branch of the NGO was pretty small though,
so it'd be weird if Cass wasn't working on the video side
of the new site. I wondered if she was still mad at me
about things with Janice. She'd looked pretty furious in
the park.

"Kate, are you OK?" Marla asked, staring at me.

"Yeah! Sorry! I was just..." I looked at her blankly,
still not quite processing the news.

"You're already thinking through design concepts
aren't you?!" Harrison said, "I can tell." He turned to

Marla, "See, I told you. She's perfect! If only all our employees were so enthusiastic and creative, eh?" He winked at me and I realised that his hand was back on my arm. Did Harrison know I was gay? He must know. But then, it's not like I ever brought a girlfriend with me to after-work drinks, and Harrison and I never really made small talk in the tiny office kitchen so maybe he just hadn't figured it out. I really hoped that he wasn't giving me the project for the wrong reasons. I shrugged off his hand and started rummaging in my bag, trying to think of something that might seem essential to reach for in that moment. I got out my notebook and jotted down some gibberish.

"Sorry! Just. Well. You know. You have to capture these things as they come to you, otherwise you never quite remember them right later." I smiled ingratiatingly at the pair of them and they simpered right back at me. I needed coffee. Lots of coffee.

"We have a client meeting later this week and, in the meantime, I'll send you all the stuff that we've talked about so far and maybe you can work with Dan and Abby to get a few ideas together. They're going to be your underlings for this project. That's cool, right?" I nodded. Dan was a nerd of the highest calibre, incredibly good at finding errors and fixing them. Abby was a tea-dress wearing, fresh out of design school, hot to trot creative whirlwind. Super cute but super straight too, alas. I guess though, if I was going to be having underlings, I needed to develop some professional managerial boundaries now. Shit. With job security came great responsibility.

Harrison talked me through some of the project's details and then I spent a while with my team. I had a team now. Then I was in desperate need of something better than the office coffee sludge and so I told everyone I was going to work from the café for the rest

148

of the day.

I sent Cass a text about the project, to let her know that I was excited to see her work and have an excuse to go for boozy business lunches together.

Cass still hadn't responded to my excitable texts by the time I got to Our Town. Hanna was behind the counter and she looked worried as I approached. "What's up?" I asked and she nodded over to the corner near the piano.

"She's been here for about three hours and she hasn't said hi or done anything but write in that angry little black notebook. Did something happen?"

"Not that I know of," I said as I looked over at Cass, her body hunched protectively over the precious notebook. She was scribbling furiously and hadn't even looked up so as to see me. "At least, that is, she hasn't said anything to me. She may have been a little put out the other day in the park. I, er, ran into her with Janice." I raised my eyebrows.

"First thing in the morning, eh?"

"Yup."

"So you're still shtupping her?"

"Hanna!"

"Well?"

"Well. Yes. I am. We are. And so we went to the park together and we ran into Cass and, hmm, it was a bit frosty I guess."

"What does that mean? You haven't spoken to Cass since?" Hanna handed me a mug of the dark roast and then poured in a dash of soy cream. It was nice getting personal barista attention.

"Thanks." I smiled at her and then gave her a full run-down of what had happened in the park with me and Cass and Janice.

"I don't know, Kate, it seems like maybe it wasn't you she was jealous of when we hooked up."

"What do you mean?"

"I mean, now she's jealous of Janice, doofus." I carried on staring at her, discombobulated. "Kate, Cass likes you. That's why she's being so fucking weird. And, obviously, she's totally not used to women turning her down so she's now completely stuck as to what to do. She's got no game and she knows it. She -"

"Hanna, please stop talking," I said. Things were starting to sink in and make sense. I realised that Cass might be hurting, and that felt unbearable. This thing with Janice needed to stop, and I needed to figure out how I really felt about Cass. Why hadn't she said anything after Hanna and I broke things off? We'd been having such a great time as friends and she'd had plenty of chances to let me know how she felt. Was Hanna just stirring things up? Surely Cass wasn't actually interested in me.

I would just go over and talk to her and sort everything out. Maybe the reason she looked so glum was completely unconnected to me. Somehow, though, I knew that it wasn't. Cass had been jealous of Hanna. That's why she had kissed me. That's why she had avoided me, and why she'd been so quiet in the park, and now she was here, writing some terribly sad epic poem about lost love.

If I could just get her to open up and really talk to me... but that just wouldn't happen. She was so stubborn, so proud. And if she was this bad at letting me know how she felt then how could we ever hope to have an actual functioning relationship. No, she had to figure out all her shit first otherwise I was in danger of just being another conquest, too easily won and too easy to throw away afterwards. I would stick this one out and let her come to me. Even if it felt like my heart had just walked out into the damp grey fog of Vancouver. Anyway, first I had to sort out my own stuff with Janice.

"Are you going to go and talk to her then?" Hanna asked.

"Yeah. I guess. But I don't know what to say."

"Well, it seems pretty simple to me. Either you like her and you tell her that, or you don't and you tell her that."

"Thanks. Great," I said, furrowing my brow. "I have to decide what to do about Janice though first." I whispered to Hanna, "The sex is really good."

"That's great, but did you really think things were going to work out this time with you guys? I know how these rebounds are, believe me." Hanna was right but I still felt torn about Janice. I did love her, but that just wasn't going to be enough and it needed to stop, whatever it was. Not being able to tell your friends who you're fucking and spending basically all your time with is usually not a good sign for the longevity of a relationship.

I decided I was going to ask Janice out for dinner. Somewhere downtown maybe. A place where we wouldn't run into anyone we knew but which also was not near a bed, or a couch, or a kitchen table, or, well... somewhere public. I told Hanna that she was right and that I'd be breaking things off with Janice. I swore I'd be single until at least 2020.

She raised her eyebrows, then nodded over my shoulder and said, "Now's your chance."

Janice was walking towards me, taking a brief look around to see if there was anyone she knew. She gave me a hug and kissed me on the lips. I grinned at her stupidly, not able to help myself. The sudden scraping sound of a chair against the floor caused me, Janice and Hanna to look over at as Cass practically knocked people out of the way to get to the door. She reached the exit before she could get her coat on. It was pouring outside. Her flannel shirt was going to get soaked through, I thought.

"Ah. Oops." Hanna gave me a thin smile. "I think

you just made things worse."

"Kate?" Janice looked at me, frowning.

"It's nothing. Coffee?"

"Er, sure, thanks. Actually, can I have a decaf matcha latte? I'll go grab us a table." Janice bounced off and I turned to find Hanna barely restraining a smile.

"She'll have a decaf matcha latte, eh? Yeah. Good luck with that."

"Hush your snark. Her trip brought her inner peace and shit and now she doesn't want to pollute it with caffeine is all." I managed to keep a straight face as I said this, but then Hanna and I both cracked up.

"And, what, you're trying to get a little of her inner peace are you?" I contorted my face into an expression of disgust as Hanna apologised. "Too far, sorry. I'll bring her drink over. In the meantime, you need to think about what you're going to say to Cass."

"Jeez. I don't know. Did she really have to behave like that just now? I mean, why storm out like a child throwing a tantrum. Can't she just talk to me like a normal human being?"

"People do stupid things when they're in love, Kate." She smiled and winked at me as she said, "Barista wisdom, sweetheart. On the house."

CHAPTER TWENTY-ONE

I was watching the *X File*s while Em hid behind her spread-eagled fingers, exclaiming that her nightmares would be my fault. "You know I have to sleep alone in that scary apartment where the bug screen rattles in the wind and the rain drums down on the skylight right over the bed. Why did I let you talk me into this?" she said as Eugene Victor Tooms's face leered in through the bars of the couple's window, Mulder oblivious outside.

"You wanted to watch it!"

"No. I didn't. Really. Why aren't we watching kitten videos on YouTube?"

"Because," I said.

"Oh, really. Really?" Em threw a cushion at me and then realised that she'd lost something precious to hide behind and so grabbed Jupiter and buried her face into his neck. He looked at me suspiciously, wearing the glazed expression he always had upon being woken from a nap. He opened his mouth and panted slowly, then tilted his head back to see what was going on with Em. When someone buried their head into his neck it usually meant they were sad and that there were salty tears to lick away. He was disappointed to find Em was just scared, so he wriggled free and took himself off to his bed. Em put her arms out, palms to the ceiling and said, "Well, you're no good, dog. Thanks a bunch for looking out for Aunty Em."

"Are you serious about being scared at yours?" I said, trying to figure out which row of my knitting pattern I was on. "You're welcome to stay over if you want. It's getting late anyway. You'll just have to play rock, paper, scissors with Jupiter for the bed."

"Scissors, huh? You'll be lucky."

"Shut up." I poked Em's knee with my knitting needle. "Seriously though, stay if you want. I promise not to seduce you."

Em snorted and then told me to hush as she leant forward to the TV, eating up Scully with her eyes. How many of us had experienced the gay awakening with that red-haired, power-suited sceptic? I, for one, had pretended to at least like Mulder for a while but gave up on even the pretence by about nineteen. Sorry Fox. Team Scully all the way.

My phone vibrated next to me, and I checked my messages, dropping my knitting to my lap. I had sent Janice a text just after dinner, asking if we could meet tomorrow morning to talk. Her reply read, "Dog park at 7?" I found it rather endearing that Janice knew my schedule, and was relieved that the message didn't seem to belie any anxiety, even though tonight was our first night away from each other since we'd hooked up again. Maybe she had an inkling of why I wanted to talk. Maybe she had also begun to realise that we'd both been clutching at something in desperation, but that it wasn't meant to be. I had failed to break things off with her after meeting at Our Town as we'd ended up back at Janice's, not doing anything as prosaic with our mouths

154

as talking.

It needed to be over though. It wasn't healthy, even if the sex was so much better than it had been when we were first together. I figured it was a bad idea to meet at the dog park though, we might just run into Cass again. I suggested a crappy little yuppie place in Kits in which no one I knew would voluntarily set foot.

I also sent Hanna a text, asking if she wanted to go for a drink after her shift. I wanted to suss out how interested she was in Em, so I let her know we were watching scary *X Files* and that Em was being cute by hiding behind Jupiter in terror.

After a few seconds, Em's phone beeped and she laughed as she checked the message. Showing me the screen I saw it was from Hanna: "Scully's a medical doctor, you know." We both drank some of our whisky and realised we hadn't been playing the game. In fact, did Scully even say that she was a medical doctor in this episode? Maybe not. Still, Hanna's reminder had allowed us to drink, thankfully.

"So you have my ex-girlfriend's number, huh?" I teased Em and she blushed but smiled. She was incredibly sweet when she was in love.

"Sorry."

"Hah! Don't worry. You know it makes me pretty happy actually. I feel a bit bad about things with Hanna, but I think it will all work out really well for you guys. You know, once you and Steve actually talk about details and stuff."

Em sighed, "Yeah. How do you even have that conversation?"

"You just do. Be honest about what you want. Set up some boundaries. Be prepared for those boundaries to change and know that you love each other and can always go back to just being the two of you, if you want." I carried on knitting, then realised I'd purled the wrong

155

bit and had to unravel a row. Knitting was like my version of having car conversations with my mother when I was younger. She would drive and I would look straight ahead and we would talk about things that were impossible to talk about in any other context. If we sat staring at each other, drinking tea, the words would seize up and die from lack of oxygen. In the car there was no way out, but conversations had a time limit, and an immediate distraction was always available. Now I knitted, giving myself something to focus on while working out what to say next. Even if that meant that I dropped stitches. It was arguably safer than driving. Stitches, unlike limbs, are a little easier to pick up once lost.

"So, do you think Hanna knows what's going on?" Em asked. "You texted her just now, right?"

"Yeah. I'm pretty sure. I mean, she's probably confused because she knows you're not single but I'm pretty sure she knows you like her and I'm very sure she likes you and I'm even surer that this is all going to work out swimmingly for all three of you."

My phone vibrated again and I expected another message from Hanna but this time it was from Kerry. She said that she was at Brassneck and had just spotted Cass. I texted back, "Who's she with?" and immediately regretted asking.

Kerry's response made me a little worried: "No one. She's just drinking by herself and writing stuff in some notebook." A second or two later Kerry sent another message asking, "Should I say hi?" I told her not to, and then asked Kerry to let me know if Cass left before her.

"Em, I'm going to walk Jupiter over to Brassneck. Kerry just spotted Cass in there on her own so I thought I'd walk by."

"Is that a good idea?" Em looked concerned.

"I just, well, I guess I just kind of want to see her,

156

you know."

Em frowned at me. "Maybe it's best to leave her be. Anyway, Jupes seems a bit sleepy for such a walk."

I knew Em was right, although I really wanted to check on Cass. I was worried about her. She'd been so weird in the coffee shop and she hadn't been in the park so I'd not had a chance to talk to her in person. I didn't want to just call her and ask flat out if she had feelings for me. I didn't know if she had anyone to talk to though, not about this kind of stuff. At least, that is, not anyone who wasn't high or trying to seduce her. It must be weird, I thought, having to navigate life knowing that, first and foremost, so many people wanted just to hook up, not even to be friends. I could see why she seemed so nonchalant about relationships; so unfeeling and uncaring. Somewhere though, I figured she must care really. She had just been treated like an acquisition, an educator, a father figure, so often that she had closed herself off. Then again, what did I know? She had only made herself vulnerable to me because our dog park relationship was simple. At least, that is, until recently.

I nodded at Em, "You're right. I'll just walk Jupes round the block and let her be."

"I think you need to, hon. She's probably working through some crap and it's best you stay out of her way while that happens. Sort things out with Janice first at least. And maybe you can talk to Hanna and suss her out a bit?"

"Priorities, huh?" I laughed at Em.

"Yeah. I'm all, like, me me me," she said quietly.

I called Jupiter and got his leash, then pulled on my coat, hat and gloves and thought again how cat people had it easy when it came to holing up for winter. No mittens with kittens.

When we got back from our walk, Em was waiting
157

anxiously at the apartment door. She thrust my phone at me, which I had left on the couch without realising.

"What's wrong?" I asked Em, unlocking the phone and then biting my lip. Kerry had texted again. She had just seen Cass talking to Manda, the lady I'd actually managed to go on three dates with before the great Scrabble-hating reveal. According to Kerry, Manda was being pretty flirty with Cass and they looked like they were leaving together.

I wanted to text Cass and tell her that Manda didn't read, that she hated Scrabble, and that it would never work out. Thankfully, I hadn't drunk anywhere near enough whisky to text such a thing.

Kerry's text cascade continued. I sighed in relief as she reported that Cass had shaken Manda off and was sitting alone again. It wasn't like Cass to disengage from flirting, especially with someone as cute as Manda.

This sideline reportage was making me feel crazy. I wondered if Cass knew that Kerry was there, watching her every move. I felt decidedly creepy and told Kerry that I didn't want to know anything else about Cass's movements.

For the next hour I sat, stewing, while Em did her best to distract me with more *X Files*. Finally, Kerry texted to say that she had just said goodnight to Cass, who was cycling home, totally sober. They had had a pretty good talk, she said. Maybe those fifteen years Kerry had on Cass had proven useful. I was itching to know what they'd talked about though. Maybe they had talked about me.

CHAPTER TWENTY-TWO

I was startled awake from my afternoon nap by a text from Steve, although it took a while that it was he who was messaging me as my phone was firmly lodged underneath a bewildered looking Jupiter. My hapless dog had woken up but failed to move. He simply lay on the bed looking unnerved as his body vibrated and made chiming noises every so often.

I wrangled the phone from beneath the beast and immediately wished I hadn't. Steve's messaged simply asked, "What's going on with Em?"

This left me in something of a quandary. Steve was due back in Vancouver tomorrow evening, and I was glad for it. The last couple of weeks had been tough for Em as she'd been trying to keep her distance from Hanna, not wanting anything to happen until she and Steve had talked.

I, of course, hadn't said anything to Hanna about Em's feelings for her, and Hanna hadn't said anything more about Em. I had the distinct impression though that Hanna was waiting to see if anything might happen, and it was excruciating to watch the two of them dance around each other. At least Hanna and I were rapidly becoming good friends. If things worked out with Em we'd be seeing a lot of each other, and that would have been awkward if there had been post-fling bitterness.

Inevitably, even from 3000km away, Steve had sensed something was going on with Em and now he was trying to suss out what he would be facing once he arrived home.

Goddamnit Em, I thought. Considering she twisted words for a living, shouldn't she be better at keeping up a front with Steve? I guess love just doesn't work that way. I wished that Em and Steve would just talk already so I could stop having to keep secrets. Maybe then everyone could get on with being happy. Everyone that is, except for me and Cass.

Afternoon naps always made me cranky but I had felt so exhausted this afternoon as I'd worked late last night on a project due first thing this morning. When midday rolled around I had realised my eyes were losing focus and I had been daydreaming that I was little spoon. I had looked over at Jupiter and told him I was just going to rest my eyes for a spell. This was always my mother's phrase. She was just resting her eyes. She was just resting her legs. She was just resting her sense of propriety and decorum. My mother had a habit of telling fantastically filthy jokes. She had also given me some great pick-up lines but I think the ability to use them must have skipped a generation.

Now, post-nap, my brain felt decidedly fluffy, and my mouth gross and sticky. Steve was asking me about Em and I didn't know what to say.

Steve was a sweetheart. Em had met him at a work function and was instantly smitten. I could sympathise; he's a damn handsome guy, incredibly tall and with the bearing of a Scandinavian god, his shiny azure eyes and

160

long blonde hair looking perpetually post-battle. Recently, he was sporting a blonde beard, peppered with gold and ginger, and I had spent many an evening resisting the urge to tug on it like a small child. After I'd gotten to know him better we'd developed a kind of sibling adoration where I would pummel my fists into his hulking great chest and he'd pick me up and spin me around and then buy me hot chocolate while I told him about my life. Steve felt safe and it had been a while since I'd had a male friend like that. I could totally see why Em was so in love with him and I had grown to love him too.

It was tough to think of Steve sitting in a hotel room in Toronto feeling confused and afraid for his relationship with Em. I wanted to tell him what was going on, to prepare him, but that wasn't my place, so I sent a text saying that Em was busy with work and maybe had just been a bit wrapped up in stuff going on with me. I added that she missed him and was just feeling a bit lonely and tired.

Steve would be back tomorrow and then they'd figure it all out. It would all be fine. It had to be. They were Em and Steve, so it'd all be cool. I realised that I relied on these two to model a solid and happy relationship, to show me that such a thing was possible. I wondered if they ever felt that pressure.

I also sent Em a message to let her know that Steve might need a little more attention. She replied simply saying, 'Arggh,' which wasn't a great help. Em had spent the week reading *Opening Up* and the *Ethical Slut*. It was her style to treat any major life decision as a research project, so she'd been scouring online poly forums and had turned up at Our Town the other day with books littered with post-it notes. She even showed me some kind of questionnaire she planned on foisting on the unsuspecting Steve and it had taken a little while to get her to realise that she needed to rein things in a bit, to let

161

Steve catch up with her. She had that glistening-eyed zeal I recognised from the days before she had quit her old job, broken up with Fran, and moved in with Steve. If we were ever to play poker I'd know her tell instantly as she could keep almost perfectly calm except for those glossy eyes fierce with enthusiasm.

It was mid-afternoon now and I knew I couldn't ignore the pile of work emails that had landed in my inbox while I napped. Rifling through them I saw I had another email with no subject line but a sender listed as Cassandra McAndrews. Cass. No one called her Cassandra, or Cassie even. I realised that I hadn't even known her surname until now, and could've easily just disregarded her message as spam.

Kerry must have given her my email address. I took a deep breath and clicked to open it.

Dear Kate,

I'm sorry for running off the other day, and for that night at the Cobalt, and for all the times I have not treated you with respect. Perhaps, given time, you'll understand why I did what I did, not that that makes it any better.

I don't expect you to forgive me, and I don't expect you'll want to talk to me again, but I really hope things go well for you with Janice.

I think you can probably see that I need to work some things through and need some space to do that. I've accepted an offer to do some filming in Amsterdam with JBD, so I'm leaving tomorrow.

Hobbes is going to live with my sister in PoCo. Give my love to Jupiter and take care of yourself.

Sorry,
Cass.

162

She was leaving. I hadn't even had a chance to talk to her, to work things out, and now she was leaving. Was this what Cass and Kerry had been talking about? Had Kerry told her it was best if she left? I was suddenly furious with Kerry and started to call her to demand to know what she had said, but I stopped, realising it wasn't anyone's fault but mine, and Cass's for not being honest and upfront. If we had just talked.

Instead, I had been the one to push Kerry to talk to Cass. I was the one who had wanted Cass to have someone to talk to who wasn't me and who didn't need anything from her. Maybe the flippancy of our conversations had led her to think that I couldn't talk seriously about things, that she couldn't tell me anything real.

It wasn't Kerry I needed to confront, it was Cass. Would she even be home now? If she was leaving tomorrow then she had probably already ditched her apartment and might just be in PoCo or heading down to Seattle for a cheaper flight. She hadn't said in her email how long she was leaving for, but if Hobbes was living with her sister that made it sound like she had no return plans.

I had to see her, so I jumped up and called to Jupiter, "Walks! Get your leash." Jupiter ran around me excitedly as I pulled on my boots.

As we marched over to Cass's place, I prayed she was still there. Maybe she was still packing up. She wasn't the most organised. Perhaps she had lost her passport beneath all those empty beer cans, packets of Drum, and Ancient Greek mythology textbooks. Her place always seemed to be in disarray, and now I was counting on that to keep her in town a little longer.

My optimism dwindled as we arrived at the front of Cass's place. The curtains were open and no lights were on inside even though it was another grey day in

163

Vancouver. I walked up to the window of the basement suite and cupped my hands around my eyes as I peered in. The glass was freezing and steamed up as I sighed. The little room was alarmingly neat. All Cass's books were gone, the coffee table cleared of ashtrays and beer cans and sushi boxes. The ragged, squishy couch was gone too and the broken sofa bed and its supporting stack of books had vanished.

Cass was gone and I had missed my chance to tell her that Janice and I were over, that I had finally realised that it was Cass I loved, that it was her I wanted, just her. I had convinced myself we had just needed time, that things would magically work out even if we never really talked to each other, and now she was leaving and there was nothing I could do about it.

I turned around and slumped onto the window ledge, tears rolling down my cheeks. Jupiter pressed his head to my hip and looked up at me, wagging his tail with cautious optimism. "We lost her Jupes. We waited too long, and we lost her."

CHAPTER TWENTY-THREE

I returned home from Cass's old place and fallen into bed to hide under the duvet. Em and I had dinner plans that evening, but now that Cass had left I felt like I just wanted to stay in bed forever, or maybe climb into a hot bath and sink beneath the water to drown out the world. Em needed to talk about things with Steve and Hanna though. A kind of pre-return game-plan.

I gave Jupiter his dinner and had a quick shower to wash off the lingering odour of nap sweat, despair and sadness. I decided to buy Em some flowers as this was Steve's Friday tradition. Em always said it was wasteful, but I knew she actually loved it. Steve and Em were both pretty great at figuring out what the other really meant, under layers of opposition. I wondered if I would have ever reached that level with Cass, who seemed to be all prickly defiance. Maybe Cass had her tells, like Em's shiny eyes, and I'd just failed to spot them.

I picked out some gerbera and a few tulips, avoiding the lilies as Thunderpuss liked to scour the countertops for anything that looked remotely edible. As the woman wrapped the flowers and handed them over to me, I glanced up at the mirror behind her and was sure that Cass had just walked by. I turned, but she was obscured by the wall of artwork in the centre of the mall. I hastily thanked the lady for the flowers, didn't wait for my change, and set off running past the guy painting a child's portrait from an unhappy looking school photograph. I crossed to the other side of the precinct, sidestepping an old man with a cane and apologising profusely as he mumble-swore at me without even looking up from beneath his baseball cap. I apologised again and scanned the mall for Cass, moving forward through the crowd of shoppers. I strained to hear the jangling of Cass's boot buckles, or to smell the mix of her tobacco and mandarin scented shampoo but the mall was a wash of sounds and smells and I cursed them for flooding my senses and preventing me from finding her. I tried to think what she might be picking up last minute before flying out, and looked into every store as I walked past.

Catching another glimpse of her at the far end of the mall I ran to the door to the parking lot, pushed past a group of teenagers and barely registered when they laughed at me. I ran past one of the mall security guys and spotted Cass halfway up the parking lot stairwell. I yelled after her but she didn't stop or turn.

Sprinting up the stairs I finally reached her at the top and grabbed her shoulder to spin her around. It wasn't Cass. I'd been chasing a teenager, a boy, some hipster kid in Cass's clothes who was about a half foot shorter and who looked both perplexed and pissed off.

"Dude," he said, "what's your damage?" Then he walked away as my arm dropped and some more petals fell off the bedraggled flowers.

Fifteen minutes later, I arrived at Em's and handed her the forlorn flowers. "Um, thanks? What happened to

166

you? Sheesh," she whistled quietly through her teeth as she looked me up and down.

"I was just walking briskly, " I said, not wanting to get into things as this evening was about Em needing to talk, not me. I handed her the bottle of wine that I had somehow managed not to break in my mad dash around the mall. "Drinkies?" I said, choking slightly on the word as I realised it was a Cass-ism.

Em laughed at my foolishness and said, "Sure. Dinner will be about half an hour so let's sit." Em fought with the corkscrew as I looked around her and Steve's apartment. She swore under her breath a couple of times and then there was that happy little popping noise and a relieved sigh, followed by the swirly glug of pinot grigio into wine glasses. Em was another of my friends that had progressed from drinking wine from jars to actual glasses. She even had a liquor cabinet these days. Steve liked his brandy. I counted three different types as I stood in front of this new living room feature. Em sidled up beside me, handed me the glass and gestured at the dark brown unit with a shiny glass front. "Steve likes his booze to have a nice place to live."

"You mean to hide from you?" I said and noticed that there were even special brandy glasses on the cabinet's upper shelf. "Jeez, Em. When is he getting the overstuffed armchair, lap blanket and a whippet?"

"Oh hahdee ha ha. You're just jealous."

"Obviously. Booze doesn't stick around long enough at my place to require real estate this good. Come to think of it, you drank the last of my gin."

"Sorry. But, hey, you'd had a tough night if I recall, so it was only right."

"True. And you had brought limes over."

"What are friends for if not to prevent scurvy?" Em laughed and curled up in the corner of the L-shaped sofa, pulling a cushion into her lap and beckoning to

167

Thunderpuss. He stomped across the room to say hi, trying to curl around my legs but finding that his enormous girth prevented him from doing so. I had to widen my stance to give him room. He almost reached my knees. It skewed your perspective to see a cat this big, especially a tuxedo cat. If he'd been a ginger cat it really would have been like living with a lion cub.

Thunderpuss followed me to the couch as I sat next to Em and asked what was for dinner. It smelled great and my belly was beginning to get the right idea now that my anxiety had abated after the hot pursuit at the mall. I tried not to think about Cass, but it was impossible. I really didn't know what else I could do if she'd already left her house. I had tried to call on my way to Em's but all I got was her voicemail. Not knowing what to say, I had just hung up. Then I'd texted Kerry to ask if she had known Cass was leaving. I didn't expect to get a reply until later, as Grace and Kerry were at some work function tonight.

I turned my attention back to Em, who had been saying something about a cashew casserole thing she was making with coconut milk and cardamom. She had stopped speaking for a moment, realising I was thinking about something other than dinner.

Em waved her hand across my face and said, "Hi. What's going on in there tonight?" She poked me in the forehead, just between my eyebrows and I grabbed her finger and then clasped her hand in mine.

"Nothing. Sorry. I'm a bit tired is all. I worked late last night on the McAllan project. It was due today."

"And you got it done?"

"Yup. All finished, hopefully. Well, I mean they'll want a million things changing of course but the bulk of it is done. It just needs tinkering with to, well, you know, to curve the straight lines and alter the layout and entirely switch the site structure. You know, the stuff they hadn't
168

really bothered thinking through for the project brief."

Em smiled, biting her lip. "Clients, eh!? Wouldn't work be so much easier if you could just do whatever the fuck you wanted and everyone loved it instantly?"

"Amen. It's like schools. They'd be great if it wasn't for the kids." Em gave me the look that meant this well-worn script could pretty much write itself.

She got up to check on the food, taking the dish from the oven to add in some chopped kale. I saw her top up her wine and realised she was drinking awfully fast and that there was already a bottle open on the side. She'd been drinking before I'd arrived.

"So, Em, how are you doing?" I asked. She sat back down next to me and smiled a brave little smile, like when a kid is told 'it won't hurt a bit' before a Band-Aid is ripped off.

After slowly placing her wine glass on the coffee table, Em looked up at me and was suddenly wracking with sobs. I was shocked by the violence of it, but I gathered her in my arms and kissed the top of her head, just letting her cry it out until she was coherent.

"What if he leaves me? What if I leave him? Is it just greedy? Should I not just be satisfied?" She looked up at me through wet lashes and I squeezed her hands in mine.

"What do you want, Em? What would make you happiest? And what would cause the least unhappiness to everyone else involved? These are the only things that really matter, right? It's not about greed and it's not about being just 'satisfied.' Just look at me and Janice. We could both have just been satisfied, but it clearly wasn't making either of us any happier. Maybe you need to think less about what you stand to lose and more about what you and Steve might gain."

"What do you mean?" Em sniffed.

"Well you hinted that maybe Steve..." I stopped for a second, not wanting to push things out into the open. I tried again, saying, "Maybe there are things you and Steve both want to explore. So it's not just all about you getting your needs met, right? You could both end up in a great position to have some freedom while maintaining and growing this amazing and wonderful core relationship. And you and Steve will probably even end up loving each other more because you'll know that you still want each other and are getting all your needs met rather than becoming resentful and frustrated." As I talked I began to wonder why I was so hooked on monogamy, it hadn't really worked out all that well for me so far. Still, I should probably concentrate on having at least one stable relationship before pursuing a bunch of things.

"So you don't think I'm a slutty bisexual?" Em said quietly.

I snorted my wine and it burned the back of my nose. "Sorry! Ouch. No. Jeez no," I said. "Are you worried that that's what people will think?"

Em nodded at me and said, "It already feels like a few friends sort of let me slip away when Steve and I got together so what will they think if I start seeing Hanna? That I've seen the error of my ways? That I'm having my hetero cake and eating it?"

"You guys have cake?!" I adopted an appalled expression, making Em laugh. "And what are you eating exactly?" I asked, and she laughed again. "You know what? If people are shitty about it then that's on them, isn't it? Maybe you and Steve will open things up, have some dalliances and decide it's not for you and go back to being monogamous and happy as clams." I frowned. "Sorry, happy as, er, Larry?" Was that any better? "Anyway, even if you hook up with Hanna, and Steve hooks up with Larry, and some people can't deal with the two or four or five or however many of you being happy then they can just get over it. It's none of their business. And, Em, you're an old hand at having people criticise

170

your 'lifestyle', right?"

"Yeah but maybe it just hurts a bit more when it's people in your own community who are being the douchebags," Em said, and I could see her point.

"No one has a monopoly on oppression though. Just talk to Steve. I mean, whatever you guys work out, this queermo is still going to love you and consider you part of the great big fabulous rainbow." I clinked my glass with hers and then sniffed. The wine I had snorted a moment ago had cleared from my nostrils and I could smell burning. "Er, the casserole?"

"Shit! Shit shit shit shit shit." Em ran into the kitchen and retrieved dinner. Thankfully the smoke show was the result of a little sauce having slopped out onto the element.

Thunderpuss responded to Em's profanities by leaping into my lap in a state of agitation. I somehow managed to keep my wine glass upright. He rammed his face into mine with a 'pet me' expression. Then he tried to get comfortable, but there was no way this kitty fit on my lap. I propped him up with a cushion on either side and gave his belly a rub. He purred and I called to Em in the kitchen, "I'd help, but your cat has me pinned."

Em piled up our plates with food while my thoughts flitted back to Cass. Where was she now? How long would she be away for? Had she seen that I'd called? I wondered if I could work out which flight she was on. I didn't have much work tomorrow so I could feasibly head to the airport and stake out international departures. Was that too much? Maybe, but I had to see her before she left. Perhaps it was too late to ask her to stay, but I had to at least try.

CHAPTER TWENTY-FOUR

It was eerily quiet when I arrived at International
Departures. A few families were hanging around, their
trolleys overloaded with plush toys and pink suitcases.
Small ballerinas and princesses clutched the cold metal of
the trolleys, staring wide-eyed with sleep. I'd looked
online and found that there was a flight to Amsterdam
leaving at 7.42am. Bundling Jupiter out of the door for
the quickest of walks at 5am meant that I had managed
to get to the airport in plenty of time to catch Cass as she
checked in. I still didn't know what I'd say to her when
she arrived.

I assumed Cass would arrive at the last minute and
probably only have carry-on. I always packed way too
much for holidays. Piles of books and a tonne of clothes.
I was an anxious packer, worrying about being too hot or
too cold, too casual or too formal, and wanting to avoid
having to buy new things and waste precious money that
could be used for food and sightseeing. I wanted to be
ready for every eventuality. I was also an efficient packer,
meaning that I could get a lot into a small space. The

problem was always that I would then go to pick up the case and be unable to move the thing.

I wondered if Cass would have anyone to meet her when she got to Amsterdam. Would the company provide accommodation? Maybe she'd be bunking with some hot Dutch charity workers. Cass had never been to Europe and I remember having joked about how that might be a good thing for all the European women who thought they were straight. Cass had dated a string of formerly straight women and I had wondered if she encouraged them because she sensed that they would never get serious and ask for a commitment from her. Now, here I was, hunting her down and about to ask her not to leave. It didn't really feel like I had any right to the question, but I couldn't just let her go thinking that I didn't care. I wasn't too proud to beg.

I got myself a coffee and sat down against the wall directly opposite the check-in for Cass's flight. An audiobook of *Middlemarch* kept me company for a while, but I gradually stopped listening as I was thinking about what I'd say to Cass. How could I convince her to stay? How could I make her realise I was really over Janice, that I meant what I was saying?

I burnt my lip and the tip of my tongue on the hot coffee and now everything tasted of plastic. I wished I'd remembered to bring my travel mug.

I watched as a teenage girl, around seventeen or so, tried really hard to be aloof as her parents checked her boarding card and passport and gave her another awkward hug and some last minute advice, barely maintaining their composure as they sacrificed their child to the world. I figured she must be going to school in Holland as she had a lot of suitcases, way too many for a holiday, even by my packing standards. Why, I wondered, are we so terrible to our parents as teens? They want to love us, protect us, and see us do well and we throw all

173

that love back in their face and make fun of them. My folks hadn't been paragons of perfect parenting but, damn, I'd been an ass to them. A lot of that was, I realised, an attempt at pre-emptive self-defence. They would only end up disapproving of me, or so I'd imagined, and so I'd determined to hate them in advance so I didn't care what they thought. That way I'd have armour against their conservatism. I hadn't factored in that they might just love me and all my quirks. I wanted to shake this kid and tell her to quit being an ass and make nice with her parents. She'd sure as shit miss them when she got off that plane and found herself alone, wandering down Oudezijds Voorburgwal. Suitcases are hard to manage on cobbles. I'd learnt this life lesson early enough in Europe.

Twenty minutes later and I was tired of people-watching. Cass still hadn't arrived and I'd entirely lost track of the *Middlemarch* plot. My coffee was done, my hands were cold, and my heart was lurching at the thought that Cass had left on a flight yesterday, taking an indirect route perhaps. Then I saw her.

She swept into the airport with a single backpack slung low over her shoulder, her usual coffee cup in hand, hair just the right amount of windswept and unkempt. I stiffened my back against the wall, suddenly paralysed by the idea of talking to her. What could I say that would make her change her mind? How could I get her to stay, to be with me?

Cass was staring up at the boards, figuring out which was her check-in, and still I stood against that wall, clutching it. I realised I had been holding my breath and so I forced myself to relax and exhale. Cass swung her backpack off her shoulder to fish out her passport and, in doing so, spotted me and froze, mid rummage. After a second or two she pushed her glasses up on her nose and

174

turned to get into the line for check-in. I ran towards her, the rope between us but she just kept her head down and got closer to the front of the line. I ducked under the ropes but as I reached her she got called over to get her boarding pass. I had put a hand out to touch her shoulder and she turned and said, "Just, don't, alright." Then she walked to the desk and I had to wait, clenching and unclenching my fists as she calmly checked in. I got called over to the next desk and for a second I considered blowing my savings on a flight to Amsterdam. If I could get the seat next to Cass then I'd have a solid twelve hours to say sorry. Maybe she'd fall asleep on my shoulder. Maybe she'd drool a little and we'd laugh about it and get to Amsterdam and hold hands as we walked out of the airport into the bright light of the city. Instead, the lady behind me pushed me aside, sighing exaggeratedly, and I apologised and moved out of the way.

Cass was all checked in and so she strode off towards security. I scurried after her, imploring her to listen to me. As we walked past the giant bear dressed as a Mountie she stopped suddenly and turned and yelled, "Kate. Stop following me. I don't want to talk to you. I have a flight to get and I'm leaving so just go home."

"But -"

"No. You can't say anything. I don't even know why you bothered coming. Go home to Janice and have your happy little domestic life and I'll be fine. I just can't be your friend right now. OK?"

"But, Cass, let me explain. Give me a chance to explain. The thing with me and Janice it's just -"

"No. Kate. I can't hear it. I can't be happy for you. I'm sorry but I just, I just can't. Not yet." Cass was so pale, her words barely making it past her lips as they trembled and I could see how much I'd hurt her and I hated myself for it.

175

"But, Janice and I are -" Cass put out a hand and covered my lips with the tips of her fingers. They were cold and I wanted to kiss them and pull her in to me, but she shook her head and turned and walked through security, out of reach.

I tried to shout after her but the words had been hushed by her insistent fingers so all that emerged was a whisper, "But, I love you." There was no way she could hear me now.

CHAPTER TWENTY-FIVE

There are few places quite as lonely as an airport bathroom-stall in which to sit and cry. After Cass walked through security, I had waited, hoping she would reconsider. Hoping that she would come running back to me. Eventually, I regained the use of my limbs and turned to walk back to the Skytrain. As I passed the giant stuffed bear dressed as a Mountie I was tempted to hug the creature, but he remained aloof and stuffy. Damn Mounties. Damn bears.

I didn't make it out of the airport, stopping instead to hide in the nearest washroom and sob uncontrollably. Now I was bawling in the stall and it felt like a flood of tears that would never stop. Every time I thought I was done I saw an image of Cass's pale face and felt her fingers on my lips again and the tears would fall once more.

I had to try to regain some semblance of control. I couldn't face the Skytrain like this. My face was sure to be a blotchy mess of sadness. I tried to think about something completely mundane so as to give myself a break. I thought about friends' phone numbers, licence plates, all of the passwords for all of my email accounts and bank cards, the order of the books on my top shelf in the living room. Somehow though, everything linked back to Cass. My copy of the *Greek Tragedies*, which she had pored over the first time she'd visited my place. *The Penelopiad* that she had lent me. I'd never gotten around to reading it and I knew she hated to lend out books. I'd have to mail it to her now, if I could find out her address somehow.

I cried until I actually felt dehydrated, but then someone came into the washroom and I managed to hold in my little sobs with my hands over my face, my body shaking with the effort of concealment. When they left, I let the sobs loose again, like an animal dying. Cass was killing me but it was my fault. I had messed it all up and now I was paying for my ignorance. Why had I been so afraid of admitting my feelings to myself earlier on? I could've avoided getting back together with Janice. Through my tears I saw the glint of white gold on my finger and I knew it was time to let it go. I tried to move it but my knuckle seemed swollen. I wiped my face and blew my nose then opened the stall door and went to the sink, squeezing soap onto my finger and twisted the ring from side to side until it slipped over the knuckle and into the basin. I rinsed it off and wondered what to do with it now. I couldn't give it back to Janice but I would never wear it again, nor could I give it to someone else. Perhaps it was simply a memento to be moved from drawer to drawer for the rest of my life, reminding me not of the good time with Janice but of how I'd fucked up and lost Cass before I'd even had a chance to really love her.

I felt the prickle of tears again and so I drew a sharp breath and washed the soap from my hands and the salty lines from my face. I had to pull myself together if I wasn't going to be trapped at the airport looking like shit for the rest of my life. My phone vibrated in my pocket and I wiped my hands on my jeans and hoped that it was Cass telling me that she had changed her mind and was looking for me.

It was Em. She was wondering if I was at the airport because Steve had managed to get an earlier flight and she was coming to pick him up but was going to be late. She wanted to know if I could meet him and keep him company. Had I found Cass, she asked.

I told her that I had but that she'd left anyway and Em replied saying simply, "I'm so sorry, sweetheart. I'll be there soon for hugs." I said I'd find Steve and we'd meet her at the JJ Bean. That at least gave me a reason to freshen up and forget about Cass for a while. He would be full of tales of Toronto and his old friends there and I knew that he would be able to give me the hug I massively needed right now.

Steve's giant blonde mop of hair was easy to spot as he bounced out of baggage reclaim, heads above the other passengers. He saw me and waved, grinning and running over to pick me up. After twirling me around and making me slightly nauseous he gave me a soggy kiss on the lips, his beard and moustache soft and tickly. He'd let it grow while he was away.

"Em's going to want to shave you when she sees that bush on your face," I said.

"Nah. She loves a bit of beard. And a bit of bush, come to think of it!" He put his arm around my shoulders and we sauntered over to get coffee.

"I hear you've been having an eventful time without me. Chasing some woman to the airport or something, Em says." He dropped his bags at a table and started pulling money out of his wallet.

"It's fine, I'll get us drinks."

"Then you'll tell your big bro all about it, eh?"

179

"Promise."

"Alright. Mine's a soy Frappuccino." He held my by the shoulders and then gave me another hug and went back to rearranging his bags.

I filled Steve in on recent events and he gaped at me until he said, "So you think you love this one, eh?"

"I do love her. I really do. And I've been such an idiot about it all."

"Well, Kate, really now. You can't blame yourself for not knowing what you want, especially if Janice was back on the scene and there's this hot barista involved and, Em tells me she's a drummer?" He was tapping his fingers against the table-top and I wondered what else Em had told him.

"Yes. She's a drummer and a barista. A lovely lady of many talents," I said carefully. "Hanna's really a very sweet person and I'm really glad that we've ended up friends. It could've gone badly but she's awesome and kind and -"

"Oh, yeah?" Steve cut me off, asking, "So you and Em and Hanna have been hanging out a bit?"

"Yeah, some. We all get on pretty well. I know you'll like her." I wanted Em to hurry up already so Steve would stop this line of questioning.

"Kate, what's going on?" Steve looked down at his coffee and licked his lips, leaving a tiny trace of spittle on the ends of his moustache. "Is Em cheating on me?"

"Steve! No!"

He carried on, the flood gates open. "I can see why. I mean, I can't be enough for her, right? I try, and I know she loves me. I think she loves me, but if there's some gorgeous woman after her and then she compares her to me and I'm this big beardy dude and am clumsy and mannish and have all the goddamn privilege and none of the trials you women have then what the fuck am I supposed to do? I can't compete with that, can I? I mean:

180

boobs! Goddamnit! Boobs!"

Steve's exclamation scared a couple of older ladies sitting nearby and I hushed him, seeing how his coffee cup was shaking as he took a sip.

"Steve. Em's not cheating on you. She loves you. I promise. And, for what it's worth, she loves your beard too. And she doesn't think you're clumsy but she'd love you even if you were, which you're not. So there." I took his hand across the table and shook his fist, "OK? Meltdown over?"

He sniffed and raised his head. "Yes. Sorry. I hate being away from her and I get paranoid that she'll leave me. I really wouldn't mind if her and this woman had something going, you know. I just don't want it to be behind my back."

"I promise. Em's not doing anything behind your back. She's an angel. And she loves you and she'll be here soon and is thrilled that you're home. You'll see."

It seemed like Em had been worrying for little reason if Steve was already on board with an unorthodox relationship model. I was so glad that her and Hanna had waited. I thought about the ridiculous banner that Em had been making last night. She had painted 'Welcome Home Steve-O!' in a speech bubble emerging from a giant sloth scaling the CN Tower. Em had really been harnessing that libidinous energy well. It was an impressive sign and it arrived shortly, attached to a delighted Em who bounced onto Steve's lap and covered his face with kisses and then thrust his head into her cleavage, once again giving the ladies at the next table something to be gape at.

"Shall we go home? Let's go home. C'mon!" Em picked up one of Steve's bags and he got the other and then took her hand and we all marched off to the parking lot. I hoped Em had remembered, in all her excitement, where she'd put their car.

181

Knowing they wanted to be alone together I asked to be dropped off near City Hall, close to where Kerry worked. I texted her on the way, asking if she had time for lunch as I wanted to talk to her about Cass. I had to figure out how to make things right.

While Em and Steve caught up in the front of the car, I stared out at the Vancouver skyline. I loved the drive back into the city, it always made me feel so happy to live her, close to the mountains and the ocean, in my usually happy queer East Van bubble.

Kerry arrived at La Taqueria in her full work attire, the crisp lines of her subtly pinstriped button-down and her shiny Oxfords an odd contrast to the skull motif t-shirts and skinny black jeans she wore outside of the office. We hugged and found an empty table. Kerry immediately got a server's attention, ordered a coffee and something to eat and then gestured at me, not even giving me time to look at the menu. To me, her order had been unintelligible, but our server clearly understood as he nodded and hurried away after I'd ordered coffee. I wasn't hungry. I felt like I'd never be hungry again. There was a pit in my stomach that was not going to be filled with quesadillas.

"So, what's up? Not that I don't like company at lunch, but this isn't just a random friendly visit, right?" Kate picked up the sugar, tapping it to loosen the grains in preparation for the arrival of her coffee.

"I wanted to talk to you about Cass."

"Ah." Kerry put the sugar down and folded her hands together. "You want to know what she said to me in Brassneck that night, right? You want to know if I knew that she was thinking about leaving."

"So you did know?" I was leaning forward too much and had to sit back as the guy plonked two coffee cups down between us. "You knew?"

182

"Yeah. I knew. I think she was struggling to tell if you reciprocated her feelings, and maybe she just couldn't bear to hang around while you worked your shit out."

"But, she's in fucking Amsterdam, Kerry!"

"Jeez, she's not dead."

"That's not helpful."

"Well, maybe you should've told her how you felt, if it's upsetting you this much."

"I didn't know! Not until I found out she was leaving."

"You always want what you can't - "

"Shut up, Kerry," I said, and drank my coffee, scalding my lip and feeling the pain was justified. I was being a horrible friend, as well as pathetic.

"For what it's worth, I think she really loves you, you know." Kerry patted my hand, an awkwardly affectionate gesture for her, which made it all the more lovely. She thanked our server for the food he had just brought over, and said, "Cass said that she thought she wasn't good enough for you, that you wanted what you'd had with Janice. I tried to tell her that that hadn't ended well, but she just laughed at me."

"Yeah, well, that's because it hadn't ended," I said.

"Woah! What? You and Janice hooked up again? Shit. When did that happen?" Kerry had a taco midway to her mouth and a load of guacamole fell out onto her tie but she didn't even notice.

"Yeah. We were having a bit of a thing." I explained to Kerry what had been happening with Janice as she listened intently.

"So, it's done now? You and Janice are broken up broken up, for reals?"

"For reals. Yes."

"Thank fuck," Kerry said, rolling her eyes

"Anyway, back to Cass and Amsterdam. I didn't

think she thought things were serious with Janice…"

"Hang on… Cass knew you and Janice were seeing each other again?

I nodded, and Kerry whistled through her teeth.

"No wonder she ran off then. I mean, even if she knew you'd broken up again, why would she think it would be any different from last time?" Kerry laughed and I scowled at her. "You could have been a bit more sensitive, Kate. It looks like you really fucking hurt her, and for what?" Kerry's matter-of-fact tone was not helping.

"Aaaaanyway," I said, "Amsterdam is a million miles away and I've no idea when she'll be back and she wouldn't even let me talk to her at the airport just now."

Kerry couldn't help grinning. "You chased her down to the airport? Quite the little sleuth in love."

"Yeah. Well, she's gone now. Do you know how long the contract is?"

"She didn't tell you?" Kerry frowned. "But you knew she was going so you must've talked to her."

"No. She emailed to say she was leaving and that was it. What, is it, like a couple of months or something awful?" I couldn't imagine not seeing Cass for all that time, especially knowing that she was angry at me.

Kerry put down her coffee cup and said gently, "It's a year-long contract, Kate."

I gripped my coffee cup and stared down into the oily blackness. I held it so tight that I thought I might shatter the ceramic.

Cass may as well have left me forever. A year?! What was I supposed to do? Would she even come back after that or would she like living there and decide to give up on Vancouver?

"Kate?" Kerry was looking at me with concern. "Here, eat a taco. It'll make you feel better. You look a bit pale."

I brushed away her offer and felt myself slowly settling into a cold, dark gloom.

"A whole year?"

"Yes. Sorry. Maybe you can email her or something. Patch things up."

"No. She wouldn't even let me talk at the airport. She just went straight through security to get away from me. I tried to tell her that I'd broken things off with Janice but…"

Kerry had spotted the guacamole on her tie and was busying herself dabbing at it with a napkin. "Good thing I have a spare in the office. I should wear a bib; I'm such a klutz, god."

"Kerry!"

"Sorry. Yes. What? Oh, right. So I guess Cass didn't see the point of hanging around for you to get over Janice."

"But I'm totally over her," I said, then added quietly, "It was just sex. Desperation sex."

"Classy," Kerry said, winking at me.

"Gah!" Kerry was proving to be pretty annoying and I wished I was just at home, with Jupiter, crying under my duvet.

"Look, kid, she's gone and you can't get her to come back so just learn from the experience, suck it up and move on. Yeah?" She patted my hand and started pulling notes out of her wallet. "I gotta get back to work. Sorry."

"OK. Well, thanks for meeting me. Don't forget the tie."

"Oh yeah, thanks." She hugged me and then said, speculatively, "Have you ever been to Amsterdam, Kate?"

I nodded my head. "Yeah, as a teenager. It's a beautiful place." I didn't really want to think about Cass and all the exploits and adventures she'd be having soon.

185

"Maybe it's time for a little return trip then. If you're serious about this woman, that'd be a pretty fucking sure-fire way to show her." She raised an eyebrow and then walked out, leaving me wondering if I'd be mad to even consider the idea.

CHAPTER TWENTY-SIX

Jupiter and I were getting ready to head over to Em's for Steve's welcome-home party when the buzzer sounded and startled us both. It was Hanna, so I buzzed her in and unlocked the apartment door, leaving it a little ajar while I circled to pick up my phone and keys and wallet and packed some treats for Jupiter. I would need them to entice him away from Thunderpuss, who really did not want to be his friend, no matter how hard Jupes tried to play-bow and communicate in Dog.

Hanna knocked lightly and pushed the door open, giving Jupiter a few excited ear scritches and a kiss on the head.

"Hey! I'm just heading out, sorry. What's up?" I went to give Hanna a hug and saw that her smile was faltering a little. I put down the wine bottle that I had been about to stash in my bag. "Drink?"

"Oh, but you're ready to leave. I don't want to make you late."

"No. It's fine. We were just going over to Em and Steve's to the welcome home party and -" Hanna had started crying and so I steered her to a seat at the kitchen counter and poured us some wine. Jupes was confused, were we leaving or not? I took off his lead and gave him a biscuit and that seemed to settle the matter for him, luckily.

"What's going on?"

"Has Em said anything to you?" Hanna looked at me imploringly and I wondered what was happening with the two of them. Had I missed something?

"Anything about what?" I asked, not wanting to betray Em's confidence. I still didn't know if she and Steve had even talked yet.

"About me?" Hanna asked while ineffectually, wiping away tears with her fingers.

I passed her some Kleenex and said, "Listen, so, I kind of can't tell you but, yeah, Em and I have talked about you and... It's complicated, you know, what with Steve having been away. Em's not had a chance to talk to him."

She looked up at me and smiled through the tears, "So did she tell you she likes me?"

My resolve wavered as I looked into Hanna's shiny eyes. "Well, yeah," I said, quickly adding, "But I didn't tell you that, alright!? I just don't want you to think it's all you, or that she's stringing you along or anything. She's not. She won't leave him, you know? And she won't cheat on him. She's just trying to be fair to everyone, even if it doesn't feel like it." I took Hanna's hand and thought about how funny it was that I had found her so intimidating until just a few weeks ago. I had been so scared to even talk to this gorgeous woman and now here I was advising her to hang tight until my best friend was free to hook up with her. It had been a weird few months.

"So, does this mean that Em and Steve are poly or what?"

188

"Not really. At least, well, not yet. Maybe." I laughed. "It's complicated! Of course it's complicated. Steve only got back today and so they've just been catching up, you know. And now there's this party so I don't think Em will have wanted to bombard him with anything. Can you just hang in there a little longer?"

Hanna was dabbing at her face with the tissue. She blinked to clear her eyes and nodded, laughing. "Yeah. I can wait. I just had a horrible day with customers and I realised that I really wanted to see Em and that I didn't even know if I was allowed to text her! It just felt so silly. Thank you."

"No problem. I really hope it all gets worked out soon. I know it's tough."

"You should get to the party though. Go have fun."

"You sure? You're OK?" I asked as I screwed the top back onto the wine and picked up an unopened bottle from the kitchen counter.

"I'm fine. Honestly. Say hi to Em for me though, yeah?"

"Sure." I gestured to the open wine bottle, "You want?"

Hanna laughed and shook her head. "No, but thanks. Probably best to stay sober rather than be drunk and morose."

I hugged her and we headed out of the apartment together before saying goodnight. I really hoped that Em would talk to Steve soon. It was tough seeing Hanna unhappy when things might be so very different.

When Jupiter and I arrived at Em's place, we paused for a second outside their door so that I could put party hats on both our heads and a party horn in both our mouths. I told him to stay and he froze and looked at me expectantly.

I knocked, then blew my horn as Steve opened the

189

door. Jupes promptly dropped his party horn and crushed his hat against Steve's legs. Ah well.

"Jupes!" Steve cried, "Here he is! The party can get going now!" He got down on the floor with my dog and the two beasts rolled around making mutually happy noises, "Argh agh argh argh agh!"

Em came to the door and shoved them aside so I could get into the apartment. I handed her the wine and she handed me a cocktail in exchange. I left Steve with Jupiter and followed Em into the spare bedroom where I dumped my coat on the pile.

"Em?" I called after her as she was about to walk out of the room, back to play host. "Em, just a second."

"Yeah?" She looked concerned and I wondered if I should just leave it. "Nothing. Well, just that I wanted to say thanks for being a really good friend even though I've been such a mess this year."

She frowned and smiled simultaneously and gave me an exaggeratedly enveloping hug. "Oh noodle. You're so worth it. And thank you for being so supportive of me, especially being a substitute spouse while Steve-O was away."

"You're both happy he's home then?" I laughed and Em grinned. "I wonder what you spent the afternoon doing, eh?"

Em looked shocked for a second and then whispered, "We spent four hours making dips! Bliss!"

"You're ridiculous. Steve too."

"Oh, I know. And lucky." Em took my hand and we went back out to the party.

I said hi to Grace and Kerry, and to a couple of Em's workmates who had clearly started drinking early. Jupiter was sniffing around for Thunderpuss who had, cleverly, hidden in the giant tree house that Steve had made for him as no ordinary cat house would accommodate his bulk. Poor Thunderpuss, ruler of cats.

190

Steve came over and kissed the top of my head, giving me a backwards squeeze. "I missed you!" he said.

I turned round to give him another hug and said, "I missed you too, you big galumph!"

"Did you miss the rain?" Grace joked.

"I did! My face is all shrivelled up from that dry Toronto air. I had to moisturise this beard of mine every day while I was in that infernal place. I had beard-icicles, I swear." Em reached up and tugged on the beard in question, pulling Steve down to kiss her.

I was so happy to see them back together again, although I'd miss having so much time to spend with Em. For a second I wondered if I'd ever get to see her if she also started dating Hanna, but I was getting ahead of things and knew I should just keep shtum for this evening at least.

One of Em's workmates moseyed over to me and clinked her glass against mine, which I thought was a tad presumptive. "Here's to the giant's safe return," she said and the wine sloshed in her glass as she swayed a little and raised it to her pillarbox-red lips. I remembered meeting this woman at Em and Steve's housewarming party. I had been trapped in a corner with her for a long time as she regaled me with office gossip, a considerable amount of which had been in praise of Em. It had dawned on me then, but I had forgotten to mention anything to Em, that maybe this woman had a bit of a lady-crush. Madeleine (I had finally dredged up her name from my memory) brushed some non-existent crumbs from the neck of my sweater and let her hand linger a little too long. I backed into the wall and Madeleine actually batted her eyelashes at me. It appeared she was trying to deploy a new tactic this evening: flirting outrageously with me to get Em's attention. Unfortunately, the eyelid-batting, slowed by her drunkenness, was less sultry and more comedic. I had to swallow my laughter along with some of my martini. In fact, I had soon drained it, giving myself the much-needed excuse to leave so I could get another drink.

I bumped into Steve at the bar and applauded as he juggled some limes before making me a G&T. "Steve, that woman is drunk," I whispered as he bent down to give me his ear. "She has a crush on Em and I think she's planning on flirting with me all night to make her jealous. I can just tell." He laughed and I elbowed him in the ribs. "Shh. Just, can you, well can you make sure you rescue me if she gets to be too much?"

He patted my head, gave me the cocktail and assured me that he'd look after my chastity. Then he went back to juggling limes.

I spotted Grace and Kerry hovering by the dining table which was laden with tempting dips. Grace was holding a carrot stick above some baba ganoush but then changed her mind and swooped it into the chipotle plum sauce. Em and Steve had stuck little flags in each dip, which was the only reason I knew what anything was.

Grace made some abominable moaning noises in apparent delight at the plum sauce, and Kerry looked a little embarrassed. I wondered if the noises were less familiar to Kerry's ears these days, now that they had U-Hauled and had a kitten keeping them up all night.

The irksome co-worker was suddenly beside me brandishing a smoked tofu, avocado, basil appetiser. She poked it towards my face, clearly looking to feed me in what she thought was a sexy manner. Steve, thank god, swooped in and ate up the proffered morsel, almost taking the woman's fingers in the process.

"Whew! Saved your life, Kate!" he said. "Kate's allergic to, er, what was that? Avocado, yes. Avocado. Right?" He grinned at me and then put his arm around the bewildered woman and whisked her off across the room. "Madeleine, have I shown you our collection of

192

sci-fi novels. Em and I are huge fans. Are you, no? Well maybe you just haven't read the right things yet. Let's see..."

Kerry loaded her plate up and went to sit on the couch. Jupiter was already there, making friends with Em's other colleague. This woman was trying to eat while patting my dog on the head. I knew that he was waiting for her dexterity to fail so he could snaffle up the tasty things that would inevitably fall onto his head. I did a quick inventory of what was on her plate and was relieved to see her eat the mini chocolate brownie first, leaving only minor toxins that Jupiter would, with his bulk, most likely be able to contend with should the worst happen.

"So, Kerry tells me you're going to Amsterdam?" Grace said, interrupting my thoughts.

"What? Er, no, well. No."

"So you're not chasing Cass then?" Grace smiled at me as if it would be entirely normal for me to just take off and pursue a woman halfway around the world.

"No. Amsterdam is very, very far away Grace," I said, rather condescendingly.

"I know." She still smiled at me, unnervingly. Would it really be that ridiculous? I had considered looking at flights this afternoon but I knew I couldn't afford it and I'd have to take time off work and what if she just wouldn't listen to me even after I tracked her down? I didn't even know where she was staying. The whole idea was ludicrous.

"I'm just not that kind of person. I don't pursue people on an international basis. Anyway, she's gone for a year, Kerry said."

"So? You have EU citizenship. You can work remotely most of the time, right? Why don't you just go?"

I was beginning to dislike this conversation. Grace

193

was making some excellent points that were systematically knocking down barriers to my upping and leaving and then finding out that I wasn't really what Cass wanted.

"Ah! But what about Jupiter?" I crunched a celery stick in victory.

"He can stay with us! The kitten went back to VOKRA. Some evil person was nice enough to adopt him, so we're pet-free again. Jupiter will be fine with us while you find a place to stay that allows dogs. Then we'll pack him some marmalade sandwiches and make him a little sign and we'll put him on a flight to you."

"That's just ridiculous Grace. Seriously. I'm not going to fly my dog across to Europe to try to win over someone who left the country because she can't stand to be around me."

"Nothing ventured..."

I widened my eyes at Grace and then turned away, finding a spot next to Kerry on the sofa. Steve immediately came over to sandwich me in and keep me from Madeleine's clutches. It no longer seemed necessary though as she had become engrossed in some queer sci-fi novel that Steve had picked out for her. I wanted to kiss him for finding the perfect way to distract her.

A few more people arrived and Em was kept busy taking their coats and proffered bottles of wine. Steve, oblivious to the new guests, talked across me to Kerry about some upcoming symphony event while I ate my smoked tofu and avocado hors d'oeuvres and thought about Amsterdam. I had been once, when I was fourteen. It was practically a rite of passage as a British teen; you either smoked weed or dated a stoner and so somehow, eventually, ended up in Amsterdam. If you had cultured parents then they may even have taken you on a family trip and unwittingly abandoned you to the local teen populace to absorb the atmosphere, not

194

knowing that the atmosphere was pretty smoky and rather full of older British teens and twenty-somethings.

I'd been with a group of five friends, all of whom were sleeping with each other in some incredibly complex system of relationships that weren't quite named. Still a virgin, and still pretending to like guys, I had done my best to avoid any contact other than a quick squeeze of my boobs under my shirt. One friend had tried to dry hump me on that trip though, and it may well have been that incident that woke me up to the reality that I was, after all, gay. Perhaps unsurprisingly, the guy's ego hadn't been bruised at all, he simply switched beds and found a more willing participant for his antics. I had gone out to wander the streets, quickly returning to the hostel after seeing far too many women in glass doorways in lingerie I hadn't even dreamt of up until then. It had been a revelatory trip in many ways and I wondered what it would be like to be back in the city now.

Still, it was a pipedream to go to Amsterdam. Even if I thought it worthwhile chasing Cass I could not justify the expense of a ticket and there was no way work would let me take time off. Especially with this new project that was, ironically, with the very NGO Cass was now working for full-time. She must've turned down that project because of me and that made me feel even worse because it sounded fun. It would have been so good to work on it with her.

As I was musing on the possibility of Amsterdam and Cass, Em appeared in front of me and took my hand. She pulled me up from the sofa and asked to borrow me for a second. Kerry and Steve were none the wiser as they were still engrossed in some discussion over who was now principal cello, or some such thing.

Em led me into the bedroom and shut the door. She fell back onto the bed and patted the space beside

195

her. I put down my glass on the nightstand and followed suit, then snuck my head into her armpit and put a hand across her belly.

"How's it going Em?" I asked, wondering why she'd grabbed me and isolated us.

She sighed and at first I thought it was an unhappy noise, but then she laughed. "Really fucking great." She laughed again and couldn't seem to stop, her abdominal muscles going haywire beneath my hand. I sat up and looked down at her.

"What the fuck? Em?" I was grinning at her but wasn't sure why, yet.

Finally, she calmed down and sat up to face me. "Steve and I talked." She grinned at me.

"And? And? What?" I took her hands and was already shaking them in the air.

"And he said that he'd spoken to you - thanks by the way - and that he thought it would be fun to see how things go with other people and stuff. Apparently he met some guy at the conference in Toronto and had wanted to talk to me but had totally chickened out. If only we'd had this talk before he went away he could've had an amazing conference! And I might not have had to wait to see what could happen with Hanna!"

"So you've got the green light for Hanna?" I gave Em a squeeze and she laughed.

"Yup! Like, a big fucking flashing green light with sprinkles! Steve wants to meet her, so I was wondering if it'd be cool if we all had dinner early next week. Is that weird? Will that be weird? Tell me if it is."

"No, no. That's cool. Actually, Em, Hanna was over at mine earlier because she's a bit stressed out about this whole thing. She had a rough day and she wanted to talk to you really, but she said she wasn't sure if that was cool or not. She was quite upset, but she'll be really fucking thrilled when she knows Steve's OK with things. Oh!

196

Oh! You should tell her! She'll be so happy." I was waving Em's arms around still but now she let go of my hands and looked down at her lap.

"But what would I say?" she mumbled. "She's definitely interested in me? Right?"

"Hell yes!"

"OK. So, well, so I don't know. How does this work? She knows I won't leave Steve, right?"

"Yes, Em. She knows. Hanna's cool. She just wants to spend time with you and see how things go. I made it very, very clear that you didn't want to leave Steve, that you love him and that you wouldn't cheat on him. She knows the score, you just have to all figure out what your boundaries are."

Em drank some of my G&T and then got out her phone. "Should I text her now?"

"Sure. Maybe. Well. Are you sober?" I couldn't tell with Em as she was often a stable drunk who appeared totally sober up until the point where she collapsed and threw up on herself. She seemed drunk on love, happiness and possibility now though, not cocktails.

"Yes, I'm sober, ish. Sober enough to make rational choices. Maybe I should wait to talk to Steve though?"

"You know, a little flirty message isn't going to hurt Steve if he's already said he's cool with things. And I know it would make Hanna's evening." I smiled, thinking about Hanna at home, trying to stay away from booze so she wouldn't get morose. Knowing that Em was interested and that they could see each other would make her so fucking happy. I tapped Em's phone and said, "Do it!"

"OK. OK." She took a deep breath and composed a message, but she wouldn't let me see what it said. "There. Done!" She gulped down more of my drink. "Oh, shit! What did I just do?" She began breathing really rapidly and I took her hand and held it against her

197

chest.

"Em, it's fine. This is exciting and totally OK and fine and cool. You lucky minx. You get to be in love and be in lust and then, maybe, be in love twice at the same time." I smiled at her and then said, jokingly, "You know I hate you for having all the fun, right?"

"Psht. Shut up. I hear you're going to fucking Amsterdam!"

"What?!" How did everyone seem to know about Cass and have shipped me off already? "Em, Cass might be there but I cannot possibly go. It's a ridiculous idea."

"But you love her?"

"Well."

"You do. C'mon."

"Em, just because you're a romantic suddenly, it doesn't mean you get to play matchmaker with me across the Atlantic."

"Kate, seriously. Quit being a humbug and chase something, someone worth chasing. I know you and Janice were messing around." I feigned shock and Em gave me her disapproving face. "You don't hide things well, seriously. I saw you guys in your fucking living room window the other night. You really should shut your blinds, you know." Em shrugged, "Anyway, my point is that rather than chasing ghosts you should go after the living, breathing, enticing woman that you've been pretending not to like since you met her."

"Em. Honestly. I just can't. It's not practical, I -"

"Love ain't practical."

"Did you really just say that?" I asked.

"Yes. Yes I did and I stand by it." Her phone buzzed and she squealed with delight as she saw that Hanna had replied. Then she squealed again as she actually read the message. "Oh my! This is going to be so awesome! Thank you thank you thank you!" She hugged me to her.

198

"Ah, OK. You're welcome." I wasn't sure why Em was thanking me, or if she was just thanking telecommunications. "How about we rejoin the party?"

"Yes! Let's find Steve-O." We jumped off the bed and went to go get refills for the drinks. Happily, I spied Madeleine curled up in an armchair, nursing a fresh drink, with *Spin State* clamped between her fingers. Steve gave me a knowing wink and then swooped in to grab Em, twirling his girlfriend around and then lowering her halfway to the ground before picking her up again and kissing her.

"Goddamn, it is good to be home!" he said, and everyone applauded. Steve actually blushed, his cheeks shining red in the space between blonde beard and floppy fringe.

CHAPTER TWENTY-SEVEN

Abby had drawn up some ideas for the new project and was trying to get me enthused about them but all I could think about was how I wanted to be working with Cass. I swallowed some more filthy coffee, wishing that I'd had more sleep last night. I had flopped about in bed until around 4am, tracking Amsterdam time and imagining what Cass would be seeing, eating, smelling, doing. Who she might be seeing, eating, smelling, doing. Even Jupiter had abandoned me to my tossing and turning, electing to sleep on the couch.

Cass had sent me a parcel, just days after getting to Europe. I had let it sit on the kitchen counter for an hour as I drank coffee and stared at Cass's loopy penmanship, wanting to know what was inside, but not wanting to be disappointed. There was no return address, but I knew it was Cass's writing.

When I finally ripped open the brown paper, I couldn't help but laugh. Inside were six flashing bracelets, intended for me and Jupiter, and a card from Cass saying that she must have been raving to have left without saying a proper goodbye, and would I forgive her? She said that she was sorry for having been so angry at the airport, and that she was trying to be happy for me and Janice. She knew, she said, that leaving had been the right thing to do, the only thing she could do to move on. She had enrolled in a class at the University of Amsterdam and was concentrating on getting credits for school and working for JBD so they might extend her contract.

For a few moments I felt overwhelmed with happiness that Cass had written to me, that she clearly cared, even if she had it all wrong about Janice. I festooned Jupiter with the wrist bands and we had a little dance party in the living room, until Jupiter shook off his bracelets and mine stopped flashing, forcing me to realise that my elation was to be short-lived. Cass was stuck in Amsterdam, and I couldn't uproot myself, even if my friends thought I should. Would it really work long-distance? It wouldn't be fair to either of us, not if we wouldn't be in the same city for at least the next year.

When I had finally fallen asleep this morning, it was to dream of flying to Europe, my plane crashing into the Atlantic. Cass was waiting at the airport with a sign bearing my name, but I never arrived.

No wonder I was so exhausted today. I shook myself out of my reverie and realised that I had no idea what Abby was saying to me. "Sorry, what?"

"Are you OK? You seem kind of out of it today." She had put a hand on my elbow and I noticed that this accentuated her cleavage which was already rather prominent.

"Kate. A word please." Harrison had suddenly appeared in the office and I worried for a second that he had caught me staring at Abby's cleavage and was about to fire me before a sexual harassment lawsuit could come about. Was it a reasonable defence to just say that I had

201

no interest in sleeping with Abby but that I did have an interest in sleeping with someone who worked for one of our clients? Harrison looked serious and this always made me worry. Had I done something wrong? Surely he couldn't actually be concerned about my working relationship with Abby.

I followed him to his office and sat down as he shut the door and asked, "How's the JBD project going? Is Abby helping out?"

"Ah, yeah. Good. She's great, thanks."

"Excellent. Excellent." He created a steeple with his fingers and looked out of his window at the North Shore mountains. I'd love to have his view but his and Marla's were the only north-facing offices; we all got East van views or south.

He turned to face me and smiled but this was not reassuring. He looked pensive. "Kate. It's been great having you in the office this past year or so and we really appreciate the work that you've been doing. The McAllan project in particular was a real success."

I swallowed hard. I was about to get fired and I had no idea what that meant for me. Would I get severance? I was a contractor. They might not even pay me for the rest of the month. Shit.

"So, Kate, it's been a really tough decision but it just had to be made and we hope you understand and are on board with our thinking." Harrison was still smiling, his perfect teeth ready to eat my dreams.

"Are you firing me?" I just had to ask. I couldn't take the suspense.

Harrison laughed and then smiled as he shook his head and said, "No! Christ! No! Sorry! Oh dear!" He thumped his hand down on the desk and chortled to himself. "Sorry! Hah! No, no, Kate, we want to hire you full-time, salaried, but there's a bit of a catch." He paused, but I was incapable of interjecting, so he went

202

on. "We were hoping that you might want to take on a bit more, well, a lot more responsibility. We'd like you to lead a major new team for us."

I realised that my mouth was gaping and so I closed it carefully and just said, "Uh, huh." I was unable to form real words. Clearly I was prime promotion material.

"I know we asked you to work on JBD, and that's great and all, but the thing is that we've been thinking for a while that we need some European representation for the company. We have a lot of clients with a base out there and, well, Dave and Alexis are going to start a European branch, along with a fantastic guy who used to work here but who is actually already living in Holland."

"Holland?"

"Yes. Amsterdam, to be precise."

"Ah."

"So, we were really hoping that you'd head up our creative team over there. What do you say?"

"Ah."

"Is that a yes?"

"Ah."

"Kate? Are you OK, you look a little pale? Should I, er -" Harrison started to stand up, ready to get me some water or smelling salts or something.

"I'm fine, sorry. It's just a bit of a shock." I took a deep breath and then started nodding furiously. "I'll do it! Yes. I'd love to. Thanks!"

"Great! So we're hoping to have the team all ready to start working by the end of January. Oliver's already in Amsterdam looking for office space and Dave and Alexis are figuring things out regarding relocation over Christmas. We'll help out with expenses and things and, well, do you need to consult with your spouse? You live with your partner, right? It'd be good to have a final answer in the next few days so if you need to discuss things with her then go ahead." Harrison looked a little flushed and I smiled at him. I had misread him, clearly.

"There's no one. We broke up last year so I'm free, although," I thought about Jupiter and really was worried about what I should do. "I do have a dog and I really wouldn't want to leave him. But, it might take a little while to get him papers and things."

"Oh. Well, is there someone he can stay with while you get things set up for his arrival? If you have to expedite paperwork then let us know. We really want you out there Kate and if it's just a little issue of finances then we can cover things and get you guys shipped out ASAP!"

My day had not gone as expected and I was in serious need of a time-out. I wondered if I could squeeze in a floatation tank session after work. Only this morning I had been wondering if Cass and I could somehow make things work long-distance, Amsterdam to Vancouver, for a year. Now I was being paid to go, being promoted, heading a design team, and all in close proximity to Cass, the woman I loved and who I'd do my damnedest to convince of that.

CHAPTER TWENTY-EIGHT

The lady at JBD was extremely helpful when I had enquired after Cass's local phone number in Amsterdam. I had explained who I worked for and that I needed to discuss how the project was going, even trying out the new job title of Creative Director, European Office. It sounded ludicrous, like I was a child wearing my mother's lipstick, badly. It was real though, and I had to get used to the idea that I was actually doing pretty well for myself. In fact, I was in charge of people now, so I had to be someone they looked up to. I was going to be holding interviews next week, in Amsterdam, for a junior designer. Oliver was recruiting an office manager, and Dave and Alexis were fighting over who got the corner office. I didn't care where I was in the office, just that I was going to be in Amsterdam in less than twenty-four hours. I would be so close to Cass. She would be so surprised.

That morning I had dropped Jupiter off with Grace and Kerry and had managed not to cry until I got to the elevator in their building. It was going to be a month until I'd see him again, and the company had paid a silly amount of money to get his pet passport sorted. Harrison, luckily, was a dog person and he had said that there was no way he was splitting up a family. He had two pugs, whose pictures he showed me while I packed up my desk. He was like a proud dad with his photos of Percy and Pingu; it was very endearing.

I had arranged to sublet my place to one of Steve's friends for the next six months and if I wasn't back after that then Steve and Em would let my landlord know. I'd packed up my stuff and put it in storage and now I was taking one last walk around my apartment. I ran my fingers over the holes in the walls where I had only recently hammered in nails to hang pictures. I had wanted to stay here for at least a year and I had just managed it, by a matter of days.

It was bizarre to think that I'd be in Europe tomorrow evening. I lay down on the cold floor and made snowless snow angels. This was my space and I had claimed it and grown in it and was going to come back to it as a new person, no matter what happened with Cass. The New Year was going to be eventful, adventurous, and unlike any other. If I could find Cass and make her part of that then all the better.

I left my empty apartment and locked the door, trying to commit the sound of the bolt to memory. It seemed important somehow, like an anchor. I had spent years of dreaming of moving to Canada, had finally done it and felt cemented here by Janice and now I was leaving again, partly because of a woman who I hoped to lure back home, back here.

I went to Em's to drop off the keys and say goodbye. Steve was going to drive me to the airport after we had a little farewell dinner. I had a bottle of wine in my bag, and my suitcases were already packed and waiting at their place.

I ran into Hanna as I arrived at their building, and she hugged me and said, "I'm glad I caught you. I have to rush off to work but I wanted to say goodbye and good luck!" She gave me the gentlest kiss on the forehead and said, "Go get 'em," then she squeezed my hands in hers and ran down the stairs.

Em was waiting at the front door as I arrived. She looked flushed and happy. Her and Steve had found that they both adored Hanna and the three of them were spending practically all their time together. Hanna had been perplexed to find that Steve had won her over too, not just Em, and had become the much sought after unicorn. I was glad that they were all so happy. It would have been harder to leave if things were still unsettled.

I hugged Em and then Steve joined us for a group hug. "We'll miss you, little chicken," he said.

"Hrmph," Em said, and I assumed this was a muffled sound of agreement.

"I'll miss you guys too but I'll send you updates and postcards and tulips."

"Just don't smoke the wacky tobacky," Em said, sagely. "I hear it's truly wacky over there."

"Em, sweetheart, that's old news to me."

"Psht. Still. You're a responsible adult now. All, like, European Creative Director and shit!" She grabbed my hands and whirled me around in a little dance.

"Isn't it ludicrous!?" I gasped.

"No, not really! Seems totally justifiable and fair to me!"

It was my turn to say "Psht," but Em would have none of it, continuing to sing my praises. I would miss these guys so much, but I was determined to make a success of things in Amsterdam, both in terms of work and with Cass.

CHAPTER TWENTY-NINE

I stepped off the plane in Amsterdam feeling a mixture of excitement and terror, along with some serious sleepiness. Alexis had offered to come and pick me up and I was grateful as my memory of high school German wasn't really helping as much as I'd hoped in terms of figuring out Dutch signs and speech. I wondered how Cass was coping, considering she spoke no other languages and had told me she had hated even studying French at school. I guess Cass always found other ways to communicate. Good old queer semiotics.

Alexis was waiting for me at the Arrivals gate and she went to help with my bags but I told her I was using the trolley to prop myself upright. The last week had been a whirlwind and I think the fatigue had hit as I'd walked onto the plane. I'd planned on sleeping most of the flight but the woman next to me had kept up an almost constant stream of chatter and I had ended up walking the aisles just to get away from her for a while. When she went to the washroom I'd pretended to be asleep but somehow my brain had skipped over actual sleepiness and so now I was wired but exhausted. I was also highly anxious about the idea of seeing Cass. Would I be able to convince her that I was over Janice? Would she think I had just come to Amsterdam for work, that she was incidental? Had she only said those things because she thought there was no way I'd come and find her?

The drive through Amsterdam's centre reminded me of how much I missed the history and architecture of Europe. North America had its grand natural cathedrals and panoramas but a good Roman era city wall, bathhouse, or bronze statue could really just take the air out of your lungs and make you feel pretty damn inconsequential.

Alexis was pointing out landmarks but it was all washing over me. She finally realised, laughed and said, "How about a little tour once you've slept?!" I apologised but she shrugged and said, "How about Oliver and I head over to your place tomorrow at noon and get you oriented. We'll take you into the office and point out grocery stores and such. Your place is furnished but let me know if you're missing anything and we'll track it down. We need you up to speed by Monday as we have a client coming in. I emailed you the file while you were in-flight but don't look at it tonight, just take a peek tomorrow if you get a chance in the morning."

I nodded and realised I was too tired to even feel the usual anxiety about a new client. Alexis unlocked my apartment door and held it open for me. I walked in and saw that it was impressively chic; as befits a Creative Director, perhaps. I knew I'd appreciate it more in the morning. After Alexis left I couldn't help but collapse onto the bed, kick off my shoes and exhale loudly, ready to sleep.

I lay there and it hit me that I had made it. I was here. I was under the same star strewn sky now as Cass

209

and this time I would give her everything.

Unfortunately, over the next few days I was kept so busy at work that the idea of giving Cass everything had to be put on hold. Alexis wasn't kidding about hitting the ground running.

The new client was an excitable start-up and they needed a lot of handholding as they worried about every little detail. I had barely enough time to figure out which of my desk's drawers should hold the whisky stash before the client called to discuss the drafts they were brining to the meeting

The week was filled with decisions, some important, some seemingly mindless. Myriad email exchanges with the new client eventually led me to make a serious effort to get the new office manager, Sami, on my side. I needed him to diplomatically filter my calls so I could concentrate on hiring a junior designer, otherwise I'd never actually have time to think about a creative strategy for the client.

As I walked into the apartment each night after work I would declare that this was the night I'd unpack and cook a proper meal. I still had no idea how the stove worked, and my only prospective friendship in the city was with Jordan, the pizza delivery guy. I had, however, found a local beer store, which meant that I felt like a moderately functional adult. I poured myself a glass of witbier and looked around the shiny white interior of my apartment. I missed Jupiter. I missed being woken up by his snuffles and sneezes. I missed being little spoon. Grace and Kerry had put him on webcam but he had been too confused. He kept looking behind the screen, almost destroying the laptop. They were just sending me pictures now, and I was glad he was in such good hands, although I was desperate to have him with me again. Was it selfish to make him take such a long flight just for a year? It could, of course be longer, but that depended largely on how things went when I finally had a chance to track down Cass. Maybe this was it for me now, living in Europe again after all this time.

When Friday rolled around I was desperate for drinks with Alexis, Oliver and Sami, the new office saviour who had kept me afloat this first week. Sami was an absolute sweetheart, juggling his Dutch and English and continuing to look unharried and impeccably attired and coiffed all day. He was only in his mid-twenties and he clearly loved his new job. He'd taken something of a liking to me too, which was a relief as my other colleagues were a tad straight-laced and I was worried that things were all getting a bit serious and practical. Maybe I really was missing Cass's playful influence.

I suspected that Sami could show me some of the more interesting parts of the city, away from the fancy cocktail bar which Alexis had chosen this evening. All four of us were drinking overpriced martinis on the business credit card, hot and sweaty in our suits and shiny shoes, and surrounded by dozens of other office types. Everyone was winding down, or in some cases charging up, for the weekend.

I wanted to see Amsterdam's underbelly, and was relieved when Sami asked if I had the stamina for a party. He had waited until Alexis was settling the bill and Oliver had gone to the washroom. I felt rather special to have been recognised as a potential partier. It was just a little gallery rave he said, some friends from his old job across town. He looked at me appraisingly and said that we'd have to tousle my hair a little to overcome the effect of the suit. The way he extended the 'o' in tousle was oddly erotic. I calmed my loins and happily agreed to the party before Alexis and Oliver returned.

"Back to the old bachelor pad then," Oliver said,

211

sighing exaggeratedly. "Maria gets in with the kids tomorrow so this is my last night of freedom."

"You should party then, yes?" Sami said, knowing already that Oliver was a family man through and through.

"No, no. I've got to get things in order for their arrival. Maria will be exhausted. There's nothing like travelling with kids to... well, there's nothing like it." He grimaced, then said his goodbyes and left along with Alexis whose partner was also arriving tomorrow, although it was a point of contention as to whether he'd be relocating or not. Alexis had jumped at the opportunity here, her relationship an afterthought. I could only imagine the ego bruise that would have left. I still found it hard to believe that the company had seen fit to give me the promotion, thereby giving me the chance to see Cass. It felt too good to be true.

Sami and I left the bar and walked to a nearby liquor store. He bought some tequila and I got a small bottle of whisky that fit nicely in my blazer pocket. It felt good and heavy in there as we walked down the street to snag a grey bike. Unfortunately, only one of the public bikes was usable, but Sami insisted he cycled while I sat on his handlebars, so we set off in a wobbly fashion towards the antique district down by Vondelpark.

The park was fantastic and I decided there and then that this would become mine and Jupiter's main haunt. I'd have to train him not to chase rollerbladers though, as so many people commuted that way here while wearing full-on wool suits. It made no sense. Clearly more office buildings needed shower complexes.

I could hear the party even before we hopped off the bike and approached the building. Sami raised an eyebrow at me and took a shot of tequila. He gestured at the whisky in my pocket. "Buckly up!" he said, charmingly, and I wondered if he had British relatives

212

that gave him these odd phrases that became so delicious in his Dutch mouth.

We walked into the fray and I lost Sami almost immediately as a friend hauled him into the middle of a big group of people dressed in sparkly vests and hotpants. I felt distinctly overdressed and now understood why Sami had removed his shirt on the way over, wearing just his vest and pants. I clearly needed to keep a change of clothes at work, as I hoped that Sami and I would make such parties part of our working relationship.

The gallery was incredible; part apartment, part art space, all in a converted old warehouse. The high windows spread all across one wall and opposite was a mezzanine from which hung huge white banners that formed a projection screen for a video installation. The dancers below jostled the canvas and created their own special effects.

A woman carrying a bunch of glowsticks knocked into me and giggled. She handed me a stick and stroked my hair slowly, then smiled and moved off into the crowd. I took another swig of whisky and moved out of the doorway towards those amazing windows.

After a couple of minutes, Sami rejoined me, his arm around a man with an enormous beard but not a single hair on his head. Sami's friend wore very tight yellow pants and a red vest, lending him something of a gnomic look. Sami introduced him as Aart and I could see that this giant gnome had a giant crush on my adorable office manager. Aart quickly discovered that I knew no Dutch and grew bored. He blew a kiss to Sami as he walked off to get more booze. Some languages are universal.

I asked Sami to teach me some choice phrases in Dutch and he said, "Proost!" and clinked his bottle against mine. I was already well on my way to feeling

213

tipsy and vowed not only to learn Dutch but also not to finish the bottle within half an hour of being at this party. I had no idea where the bar was, or how to get home, and there was something to be said for sobriety in a new city at night.

I spent the next couple of hours bouncing around on the dance floor, nodding attentively at conversations I had no hope of understanding, and meeting a bunch of Sami's lovely friends who spoke incredibly good English and who kept bringing me more and more drinks. By 1am my energy was flagging. The noise and the concentration, and no doubt the whisky, finally got too much, so I tracked Sami down and said goodnight.

He ordered me a cab and came outside to wait with me. As the cab pulled up, Sami gave me a sweaty hug, and I thanked him for making my first week in his city so awesome. He hugged me again and ran back into the party.

On the way home the taxi driver skillfully negotiated his way through the drunken revellers tottering across the cobbled streets. I fished in my pocket for my phone and tried to focus my blurry eyes on the screen. Eventually, I tracked down the note I'd made of Cass's address and asked the driver if it was nearby. It took a few attempts to pronounce the street name but finally he said we could take that route back to my apartment if I wanted. I wanted.

We drove slowly down the street to Cass's house and the driver asked if I wanted to stop. I stared up at the apartment building, knowing that now was not the right time to make my presence known. I needed to be sober so she'd see I was sincere. I asked the driver to take me home. I was ready to fall into bed and enjoy a weekend lie-in. The car skipped over the cobbles by the canal, and I relaxed into the seat and closed my eyes, determined that I'd see Cass tomorrow, with a clear head.

CHAPTER THIRTY

The next morning I decided to explore my new neighbourhood, taking in the brown cafés, despondent drunks, and sorrowful stoners still coming to terms with the night's demise. I made the mistake of heading down to the Royal Palace and then the streets beyond and was appalled to see a man trying to convince a tourist to pay for his trip by pimping out his wife. It was 10am and somehow the seediness of the night had slipped into the day. This city was certainly one of contradictions and complexity. Would I ever really be able to call it home?

I stopped at a book store and bought myself a Dutch/English dictionary and a bunch of Learn Dutch tapes, along with a coffee and a muffin in the bookstore café. The vegan muffin was a pleasant surprise. I only wished that all translations into Dutch were as simple as 'veganistisch.'

It was a beautifully sunny day and crowds of tourists filled the streets as I strolled around and took in the sights I'd missed all week while I had been cooped up in the office. Seeing so many cyclists made Amsterdam feel a little like home, but I missed the mountains, and not just as a simple way of orienting myself in the city.

I hadn't been paying attention to where I was going and so I looked around for a street sign and then realised that I was back on Cass's street, not far from her place. The building looked even sketchier in the daylight.

I couldn't resist loitering for a minute and staring up at what might be her window. I knew it was creepy, and I knew there was a risk of running into her. I hadn't figured out what I would say to her when I did find the courage to climb up those steps and push that buzzer. Cass had no idea I was in the city, let alone that I was right outside her apartment. She was probably in bed, sleeping off a hangover, or maybe having sex with some hot Dutch lady, assuming that I would never chase her all this way.

I was about to set off home when I saw that the door to Cass's building was slowly being opened. I held my breath, but wasn't Cass who emerged. My disappointment held me in place momentarily until I took a deep breath and resolved to come back that afternoon and see if I could talk to her, after I figured out what I wanted to say.

I did go back to Cass's apartment that afternoon and I even held my finger poised over the buzzer for a second before I turned and ran home as fast as I could. I was terrified that some other woman would answer the door and I would see that Cass had already moved on, was onto her next conquest. Maybe she hadn't ever really loved me, she had just enjoyed the drama because I was unavailable. Maybe she would still refuse to believe that I was over Janice. I just wasn't ready for the rejection. Tomorrow. I'd come back tomorrow. I'd feel better after a proper night's sleep. My mind was still too jittery from all that had happened this week.

216

The next day I went back to her building but this time I just stood on the front steps, paralysed by fear. I had come all this way and now I couldn't even climb the steps and push the intercom button. I retreated to my apartment and sat staring at the white walls. I missed home. And I missed when things with Cass had felt so easy and relaxed.

Finally, on the Monday, after a post-work drink with Sami, I had enough Dutch courage to mount those steps and push the button before sobriety and fear, the best of friends, kicked in. There was no answer. I waited for a few seconds and then I pushed the buzzer again. This time I heard someone pick up and then a crashing sound. A woman spoke some Dutch at me and I flailed around for an answer. I ended up simply asking for Cass, saying over and over that I was a friend, a friend of Cass's. There was a pause and then I heard the door click to let me in. I pushed the door and held it open for a second or two, wondering who this woman was and if I really wanted to find out.

I walked into the building and saw that the foyer was a classic example of how an austere and grand house had fallen into disrepair. The entranceway featured once beautiful tiles, now chipped, covered in plaster and cement; some sections were missing entirely. The bannister of the stairwell was loose and innumerable moving accidents had left the stairs themselves ragged with gouges from fallen wardrobes, desks, pianos and such.

The contrast between my own apartment, all shiny with chrome, and Cass's accommodations was stark. I guessed her NGO freelancer salary didn't stretch far and once again I pondered her reasons for working for them. She said that she just did her job for the paycheque but I knew that, despite her façade, what she saw all day every day on the footage she edited did have an effect on her.

Caring just didn't sit well with her well-crafted persona of not giving a shit. In her letter she had talked about being excited to start the course in international development that she had signed up for at UvA. She had even mentioned that she was considering switching programmes. It was hard to think of Cass working hard to solve the world's problems, but she had always taken school seriously, it was just the partying and the women that had sidetracked her again and again.

I reached the third floor and saw that the door to Cass's apartment was open. I knocked but there was no answer, just the sound of whirring from inside. I stepped inside, gingerly, and saw a woman in the kitchen, barely dressed, making some kind of green smoothie. She hadn't heard me over the sound of the blender and so I waited and then coughed quietly.

"Hallo! Cass's friend, yes?" She gave me a hug, despite only wearing her underwear, and offered me a glass of the juice. I declined, already feeling somewhat nauseous. Was Cass sleeping with this woman? Had she already moved on?

I introduced myself and found out that this woman, Mona, was a filmmaker with whom Cass was working. Mona asked what I was doing in Amsterdam and, after I told her, she looked around for a business card. She finally fished one out from between the pages of a recipe book, dusting the card off before handing it to me somewhat apologetically.

I thanked her and then looked around pointedly. "Is Cass here?" I asked. Mona laughed and beckoned me in to see the rest of the apartment. It was decked out with bunting and there were balloons and a cake and a couple of kegs already tapped. Mona told me that Cass was picking up more supplies for the party they were having that night. She seemed to think that Cass had invited me to the party and I'd arrived early to help so for the next

218

hour I was put to work moving around furniture and making platters of vegetable crudités. I got so caught up in Mona's frenetic activity that it didn't even occur to me how weird it would be when Cass found me in her kitchen chopping carrots. I still hadn't established the relationship between Cass and Mona, but I had noticed that there was just one bedroom.

Soon, people started arriving for the party and, as Cass hadn't returned yet and Mona was still getting dressed, I ended up playing hostess. Thankfully someone figured out music and someone else worked out a more relaxed lighting situation. Finally, Mona emerged from the bedroom looking resplendent in a long floating silver dress, her hair coiled on top of her head in a scarf and her face artfully made up. She kissed each of her guests in turn and ensured everyone had drinks. As she handed me a glass of beer she kissed me on the cheek in thanks for welcoming people in her absence. Her costume change had switched her from a semi-naked and flustered film student to a successful media socialite. It was an impressive transformation and as I watched her work the room I wondered again at the extent of the relationship between her and Cass. I could see how she could fall for Mona.

I was soon embroiled in a conversation with a British journalist and a Dutch painter over the lack of column inches devoted to serious critical art review in mainstream newspapers and I kept having to remind myself why I was even at this party. Dick, the journalist didn't seem to have any idea who Cass was and Christian appeared to think that I meant Mona's sister who had been staying with her for a while. I explained Cass was Canadian and they both looked confused and went to get more beer, clearly thinking that their sobriety was the cause of the confusion.

A couple more people arrived and, as I greeted

219

them at the door, they gave me their coats. I stood in the kitchen for a second, wondering where to put the heavy woollen jackets I had just had thrown into my arms. I caught Mona's eye and she nodded towards the bedroom so I made my way through people and nudged the door open with my hip.

The bedroom was lit by a streetlamp, the thin curtains doing nothing to hide the glare. I added the coats to the pile on Mona's bed, and turned around to go back to the party. Then I spotted Cass's pendant on the nightstand. Her ex had given her the stone pendant as some kind of talisman against evil, or confusion or some such thing. I had never seen her without it.

I felt horribly hot suddenly and so I returned to the living room, but the heat of all the people was even more overwhelming. I had to get some air, so I climbed out of the kitchen window onto the fire escape, pulling the drapes back across to muffle the noise of the party.

I perched on the cool metal and let my legs dangle out over the alleyway. I should really leave, but I just needed to get my breath back first. The sounds of the music and chatter behind me was slightly soporific and I tried to relax and let the cool night air swirl around me, bringing with it the sounds of the city.

The clanging noise of footsteps below interrupted my peace and all of a sudden Cass's head emerged beneath my feet. She stopped and stared up at me dumbfounded. I was incapable of speech or of any movement and just sat frozen, willing my brain to form the right words or to make my body move in the right way. I just wanted to hear Cass speak to break the spell but she didn't even seem capable of the typical, "Holy shit, dude."

After an interminable few seconds Cass climbed up next to me, put down her bag, got out a couple of beers, removed the caps and handed me a drink. She went to

220

take a swig and then paused and clinked her bottle into mine, shaking her head, drinking and then laughing until I could see tears coursing down her face.

Finally, she looked back at me and said simply, "Hi."

"Hi yourself."

She laughed again and carried on shaking her head in disbelief. "I'm sorry; I just can't quite believe that you're here."

"I crashed your party."

"Yeah. You really did fucking crash my party." She got out a cigarette and tapped it on her tin before lighting it.

"Happy birthday?"

"It's not my birthday, kid."

"But, the balloons?" I said. Then I realised maybe it was Mona's birthday. "Your new girlfriend seems nice," I said, and swallowed some beer, looking away quickly.

"Mona's an old friend. And she's straight. And she's kind of having an affair with my boss." Cass was grinning when I turned to look at her, and I saw that she was playing with the pendant around her neck, identical to the one on the nightstand. I smiled and laughed, thinking how it was going to be hard for us both to get used to not expecting the worst from each other all the time.

"Did you get me a present?" Cass asked, and I held up my wrist, with all six bracelets.

She laughed and took a couple of drags on her cigarette before shaking her head and then sitting down beside me. I turned towards her, my heart pounding furiously. The noise of the party seemed so far away now. It was just me and Cass, so close.

I felt Cass's fingers slide over mine, cool and smooth. She cradled my left hand in hers and looked up at me, then back down at my hand, flipping it over slowly. She looked up again, blew her cigarette smoke off high and to the right and said, "You're not wearing the ring." I nodded and Cass stubbed out her cigarette and flicked it off into the alleyway below.

She was so close. I could smell the lingering tobacco on her breath, the coffee, her peppermint lip balm. Cass's hand was shaking but it wasn't cold tonight, even out here on the fire escape.

"It was time," I said, "to let her go, you know." Cass ran a finger around mine and I looked down to where the engagement ring had been, the thin white gold band Janice had given me as a last desperate try at capturing happiness. The loop Cass's finger made around mine was gentle but incomplete, free. I, too, was shaking now and I had to suppress an urge to laugh, knowing it might lead to crying.

"Kate."

"Uh, huh."

"Look at me?"

My head felt so heavy, like the last year had tethered me to the ground somehow, stopped me from looking up to see what was right in front of me. Cass offered the softest of touches to lift my chin, and she met my mouth with hers. Our eyes open, I saw hers soften into the smile I had been waiting for since I had met her. She saw me, she touched me, she got me, and it was serious this time.

ABOUT THE AUTHOR

Leigh Matthews is a British-born writer who lives in Vancouver, BC, with a sharp-eyed border collie who is both her biggest fan and harshest critic. Her first novel, The Old Arbutus Tree, was published in July 2013.

Printed in Great Britain
by Amazon